Also by RUNE MICHAELS

NOBEL GENES
THE REMINDER
GENESIS ALPHA

FIXME

RUNE MICHAELS

ATHENEUM BOOKS FOR YOUNG READERS
NEW YORK LONDON TORONTO SYDNEY NEW DELHI

ATHENEUM BOOKS FOR YOUNG READERS · An imprint of Simon & Schuster Children's Publishing Division · 1230 Avenue of the Americas, New York, New York 10020 · This book is a work of fiction. Any references to historical events, real people, or real locales are used fictitiously. Other names, characters, places, and incidents are products of the author's imagination, and any resemblance to actual events or locales or persons, living or dead, is entirely coincidental. · Copyright © 2011 by Rune Michaels · All rights reserved, including the right of reproduction in whole or in part in any form. ·ATHENEUM BOOKS FOR YOUNG READERS is a registered trademark of Simon & Schuster, Inc. · For information about special discounts for bulk purchases, please contact Simon & Schuster Special Sales at 1-866-506-1949 or business@simonandschuster.com. · The Simon & Schuster Speakers Bureau can bring authors to your live event. For more information or to book an event, contact the Simon & Schuster Speakers Bureau at 1-866-248-3049 or visit our website at www.simonspeakers.com. · The text for this book is set in Berling. · Manufactured in the United States of America   10 9 8 7 6 5 4 3 2
Library of Congress Cataloging-in-Publication Data · Michaels, Rune. · Fix me / Rune Michaels.   · p.   cm. · Summary: A sixteen-year-old girl endures a miserable life with her aunt and violent twin brother, but when memories of an even worse past resurface she runs away to a zoo, where she finds an unlikely sanctuary and allies. · ISBN 978-1-4169-5772-0 (hardcover) · ISBN 978-1-4424-3635-0 (eBook) · [1. Emotional problems—Fiction. 2. Zoos—Fiction. 3. Family problems—Fiction. 4. Runaways—Fiction. 5. Brothers and sisters—Fiction. 6. Twins—Fiction. 7. Orphans—Fiction.] I. Title. · PZ7.M51835Fix 2011 · [Fic]—dc22 2010051490

CHAPTER ONE

The wood is splintered around the lock, where he wedges a knife to force it open. The door to my room is scarred, the doorknob dented.

Brothers and sisters fight, Aunt Phoebe says. *It's normal. It's a law of nature. Did you know shark fetuses fight to the death in the womb?*

Aunt Phoebe watches "Shark Week" every year.

I throw myself into my room, slam the door and lock it, yelling ugly words from behind its shelter. My dresser stands just inside the room. It doesn't take me long to push it against the door, but it's not heavy enough. I have to lean against it, brace my feet against the floor and push against the door, bulging open with every punch, the hail of curses shooting through the wood. Adrenaline surges through my system. The desperation of keeping steady pressure, the mad rush of fear when a sliver of light shows the door has opened enough to let in photons. After photons comes his foot, and I hurl my body at the dresser, making him bellow in pain. Sometimes that works. But this time his foot doesn't budge, and I know what happens next. The door will blast open. A kick. A punch. Until I fall to the floor. My books, penholders, everything pushed off their shelves with a few violent movements of his arms, raining down on me; nothing breakable, though, because everything's already been broken. A hand snaking through my hair, grabbing a hold. The sudden pain of the yank, my throat sore from screaming as he drags me by my hair out of the room and down the stairs. It's a dance and I know every step.

The door bursts open. The choreography has begun.

I back away, but my brother slides his foot behind my ankle and yanks. I fall. I hit my head on the edge of the desk, and the world goes out of focus for a second. Then I see the raised arm above me, the clenched fist in the foreground, the narrow wrist and the arm.

Familiar, but something is different now.

His shirtsleeve is missing a button. It has fallen open. I gulp in air and hold it as I see the red lines in perfect focus now straight in front of my eyes, one after another up the underside of his arm, precisely parallel, like they were planned with a ruler.

I grab his wrist, wrap my fingers around it and hold tight, and he pauses, because I've broken the pattern, I've interrupted our dance. My arms are supposed to be crossed in front of my face, covering my head, while his fists punch into my shoulders and arms and his feet slam into my legs. He never kicks me in the stomach or punches me in the face. It's weird. He seems out of control. But he's not. He knows what he's doing. He always does.

"What?" he growls as my hand tightens on his wrist, turning his hand slightly.

"You too," I say. "You do it too."

He looks confused. "What?"

I touch his scars. They're raised, red, recent. And underneath, the whiteness of older wounds. He pulls back. Yanks the sleeves of his shirt down and stands, his hands clenched, staring down at me.

The floor is hard against my back; my head still aches from where he pulled my hair out. I open my hands, hold out my palms. Show him what I've never shown anyone before. Lines, like his. The old white lines crisscrossing my palms, the new swollen red lines on top of them, the rough skin surrounding wounds that don't get to heal. Brian looks. Then he walks away, and I'm still on the floor with my books strewn around me, my pens dotting the floor, a head that aches, but I'm smiling, because for a moment I love my brother again.

His bike roars, the walls shiver. The roar softens into a purr before it vanishes into the distance, and I stare up at my empty bookshelves and think about the Doppler Effect.

"You shouldn't provoke him." Aunt Phoebe stands in the doorway. Her gaze flutters from the books on the floor to the empty shelves, and then she rubs her temples. Aunt Phoebe works shifts. I never know when she's at home and when she's not, but it doesn't much matter anyway. "What a mess," she says.

I stand up, start putting the books back in the shelves. I don't bother being neat, simply pile them up. They'll be down on the floor again soon enough. But the heavier ones go on the bottom shelves. That's what they recommend for earthquakes.

"You like to believe it's all his fault," Aunt Phoebe continues. "But you're to blame too. You push him until he goes over the edge. You know he will. You know what will happen, every time. Why don't you leave him alone? Why don't you just stay out of his way? Why do you yell back? Why can't you just ignore him until he gives up?"

I bite my lip. Align the books so their spines match up while I wait for her to finish her little speech.

"This isn't easy for me, either, you know that. It's not like I don't have better things to do." Her hands are busy twirling a button on her shirt. "I'm doing this for you kids. I'm doing it all for you and you couldn't care less. The social worker is coming over today, you know. Brian's school record this year—atrocious. And this reflects on me. Like I don't try my best. Like I haven't always tried doing my best for you two."

"Go, then," I mutter. *I'm staying until you're eighteen,* is what she'll say next.

"When you're eighteen," Aunt Phoebe says, and her face relaxes, an almost invisible smile tugging at her lips as she looks over my shoulder, like she can see out the draped window, toward the home she had to abandon to look after us, into a future where she's free. "We'll have to make this work until then. Don't we? Sweetie—if we all try our best . . . all of us . . ."

I hate when she calls me sweetie. It's fake. She knows that's what Mom used to call me, me and Brian both, and that's why she uses it, like using the word will make me into the sweet little kid I used to be.

She reaches out, as if to tuck my hair behind me ear, like Mom used to do too. I rear my head back and scowl at her. I'd like to kick the door shut in her face. But ignoring her makes her go away sooner.

And her hand falls down, she sighs, walks off, back to the kitchen for a smoke and coffee from a mug with an astrology sign. It's not her mug, not even her sign. Nothing in this house is hers, and she knows it. She walks around like a stranger, or maybe more like a servant, but she's not the only one who doesn't want to be here.

The morning sun pulls me outside. I stand on the porch and turn my face up, feel the warmth seep into my skin, picture the sun's radiation searing my DNA, warping it until my cells spiral out of control. My skin feels red and swollen when I go back into the house. I take a washcloth and hold it cold and wet against my skin, look in the mirror because it's safe now; my image is distorted by an afterimage of the sun burning itself into my retinas. It's safe now, because all I see is a shape, a shadow, not a person.

I'm broken.

But nobody's trying to fix me.

The social worker will be here at four. I make myself scarce so by the time she arrives, Aunt Phoebe will think I'm not around. I lie down outside the kitchen window, in a warm bed of grass, bugs crawling over my arms and legs, and inhale summer while I wait. Mrs. Foster is always punctual, always *exactly* on time, and her little drama with Aunt Phoebe has been perfected over time. Their ritual, the coffee, the tea, the chocolate chip cookies and ginger cake, their small talk about town politics before they settle down to business—to us.

That discussion, too, is familiar. First there is Aunt Phoebe's litany of complaints about us. Then Mrs. Foster soothes her.

"I'm not sure I can do this anymore," Aunt Phoebe groans.

"I understand," Mrs. Foster said. "That's what we're here for. To support you. It isn't an easy task you've taken on."

"It's getting worse. They never seemed to have recovered after their parents' deaths. I've done my best, but . . . And as they get older . . . and stranger . . . I feel like I don't know them at all. I can't connect with them at all. And I know they hate me."

"They don't hate you. They're teenagers. When they're a bit older, they'll appreciate all you're doing for them."

"I don't know. Sometimes I hear myself talk to them, the things I say, and how I say them, and I don't blame them. I don't blame them at all. They're so difficult, and I can't deal with it . . ."

"Have you given any thought to moving? It might be better for them . . . for all of you . . . to move to another house. This is where they lived when their parents died. Perhaps in another environment they will settle down . . . get closure . . ."

This I hadn't heard before.

I picture myself in another house and the picture fits, as if I'm taking a doll and moving it from one doll's house to another one. I chew on a blade of grass and feel Aunt Phoebe shaking her head. "I can't take them home. I can't take them into my home. I rented out the house, and anyway, I couldn't take them in. My things . . . Brian doesn't respect anything. He would break and steal everything I own . . ."

"You have power of attorney. You could sell this house, buy another one. I understand their parents' life insurance paid off the mortgage. It should be easy."

"That won't help. It will just be trouble. It's impossible to predict how they'd react."

A kitchen chair creaks. "Where are they now?"

"Around," Aunt Phoebe says vaguely. "She has a summer job. As for Brian, who knows what he's up to? They're teenagers. I can't watch them like babies."

"Of course not. We don't expect you to. As long as they attend school and stay out of trouble . . . and well, that is a problem, you know that—school attendance was exceptionally bad for Brian this year."

"I know. But what can I do? If you people think you can do a better job, feel free . . ." Aunt Phoebe gasps. "I'm sorry. I didn't say that. I didn't mean it."

Insects buzz around me, on me, rustle in the grass, hurtle through the air. I close my eyes and imagine I'm one of them. I fly up and peer through the screen with my multifaceted eyes, and see Aunt Phoebe and the social worker, a hundred tiny images of them, each with their cup of coffee. Hundreds of clipboards. I ignore everything and zoom greedily in on the lumps of sugar.

"I know you're doing your best. But he has to go to school. It's the law."

"I know. And as their guardian, I'm the one who gets in trouble if they decide they don't want to go. It's not fair. It's been years. I've sacrificed everything for those two for years. Nothing I do for them is good enough. Nothing I do is ever good enough . . ."

I find a rip in the screen. Coordinate my six legs, maneuver through. I know what I want. Sugar. Aunt Phoebe has dipped a lump in her coffee, then left half in the saucer, the sugar molecules warm and fragrant.

"We know," the social worker says soothingly. "They're lucky to have you."

"They hate me. I can't reach them. I can't reach them at all. I'm so close to giving up . . ."

"There, there," Mrs. Foster says.

It's the final steps in the ritual. Aunt Phoebe's tears, Mrs. Foster's murmurs of encouragement. Then tissues, a deep breath, and a brave promise to soldier on, because we're family and of course she loves us—it's not that she doesn't love us. . . .

My eyes are still closed. I land on the edge of the saucer, balance on my six feet, dip my proboscis into the soggy surface of the sugar lump, and feed.

CHAPTER TWO

I don't feel very well when I turn into the street on my bike and see the Dungeon Café sign and the smiling dough-nut logo. I park near the back entrance and take my time chaining the bike to the fence, postponing the moment when I have to go inside. My stomach somersaults as I pull the door open a fraction and squeeze inside through a narrow opening, as if I'm less noticeable that way.

"Don't be silly," Rosalyn would say. She has a new boyfriend now, one who doesn't hit her, one who doesn't wield words like razor blades, and she is happy. Brian would freak if he knew she's gotten me a job, if he knew she still likes me even though she's dumped him. Rosalyn is brave and pretty and everybody likes her, and I wish I were more like her. "You're doing fine!" she said my first day here when she found me hiding behind the Dumpster, on the verge of fleeing home and hiding inside my room. "Don't worry so much. Get back inside. Just wipe the tables, and if someone tries to order something, let me know and I'll take care of everything. You can do this. I know you can."

It's been almost a week since then, but I'm still not sure I can do this. It's even worse than school because there are new people here every day. So many eyes and at any moment, some of them may speak to me, and I always, always say the wrong thing, or don't say the right thing, or don't say anything at all, and at the end of the day I want to go home and find my box of needles and scratch until all the bad stuff leaks out.

A few of the staff are clustered in the small room at the back of the café, giggling over something on the tiny TV in the corner. I stand and watch for a while, a gossip show about rich celebrities and the silly gifts they give each other. Rosalyn notices me, gestures for me to come over, and I move closer, one tiny step after another, until I'm almost a part of their group. I feel peaceful for a few moments, until one of them looks at me. "Nice shirt," she says, smiling, and I look down at my blue-and-white shirt, an old one Rosalyn gave me. I look up at the girl's face and down at the floor. I don't know if she's being nice, or making fun at me because I'm wearing someone else's castoffs. I try for a casual thank-you, but the words tangle together in my throat, and when I open my mouth to stutter them, it's too late. They're looking away from me now, talking about something else, and I've lost my chance—I no longer have anything to say.

Relief and regret mingle, relief bigger and brighter as usual. The conversation buzzes around me; I no longer detect individual voices; the threads have merged into one giant ball of vocal yarn weaving around my eardrums. I try to fit in. I struggle to smile when I see them smiling, laugh when everybody laughs—I try to fade into the background and be invisible, but it never works.

"Okay. Break over." Rosalyn grabs a couple of aprons off their racks and throws me one. "To work, gang! We've got cholesterol to serve!"

I organize my cart, fill one container with soapy water, hang the cleaning sprays on their rail, line up the rags and towels, click the mop in its place, and then take a deep breath and push out there.

I'm responsible for forty tables. They have glass tops and chrome legs, and as soon as I've emptied and cleaned one, it fills up again. Empty cups of coffee, half-eaten doughnuts, sandwich crusts. Fingerprints smeared on the glass, spilled drops of Coke, jelly drops. Lots of cups and glasses and plates to stack up and bring back to the kitchen, where someone loads the giant washing machine. Almost nothing is disposable here because the Dungeon is a "green" café.

I keep my eyes on the glass surface, on the soapy suds I spray, the rainbow sheen when I wipe the soap off, the sparkle of clean, and try not to look at the customers, because if I do, they sometimes mistake me for a waitress and ask me for something. Nobody stays long. They're in a hurry, most of them. They're real people—they have trains to catch, taxis to hunt down, places to be, things to do. They leave tips, small heaps of coins beside their abandoned plates, but they're for the waitresses, not for me.

"Excuse me, miss?"

My heart lurches. I force my mouth into a smiling shape, look in the direction of the faceless voice, mumble my standard "A waitress will be with you in a minute," and scurry off to the other end of the café, muttering the number of the table as I pass Rosalyn. It happens all the time, of course. They don't know I'm just here to wipe tables and push the cart with the dirty dishes.

My palms burn when I push my hands into the soapy water and wring out the rag. That's important too, to feel the pain stream from line to line, a pattern of pain extending up my arms and into my brain, where I picture a corresponding pattern, a glowing maze of firing neurons spitting neurochemicals at each other.

Brian does it too.

The first time I scratched my palms, I was sure I had slivers of glass stuck under the skin. I don't know why. I hadn't broken any glass. But I was so sure I had tiny shards of glass embedded in my skin, I thought I could feel them, crouched under my skin, and I got terrified as I pictured them getting loose, getting into my bloodstream, heading straight for my heart, and killing me. So I tore through the kitchen cupboards until I found the small sewing box with needles and thread, and I chose one needle, and I sat down and picked at my palms, trying to get the glass out.

I never found any glass. But I'm still not sure it's not there.

My lines aren't as neat as Brian's. Mine are a chaotic mess; his are precise and even, exact and perfect. He cuts deeper than I do; I barely scratch the surface most of the time. His scars are thick and raised. I'm more of a coward than he is. I always was. I just like to play with needles. I like to scratch my skin, see how deep I need to go before there's blood. I don't always bleed. Sometimes I only drag the needle over my skin, barely making a mark. Sometimes I scratch over and over at the top layer of skin until it's gone, but there's still no blood. Only an ache, like after a sunburn. It's an art, scratching away the top layer of skin without causing any bleeding. I once read that surgeons practice on the membrane inside a raw egg. It's almost like that.

I curl my hand around the mop, feel the damp plastic against my palm. I focus on the sensation as I start near the door and work my way to the safe, shadowy inner corner of the café, and sometimes I manage for a few minutes not to think about anything at all.

The hours pass slowly. I play my usual game, try to avoid looking at the clock as long as I can, and then guess how much time has passed. I suck at it, but I think I'm getting better. I know now how long I take wiping down ten tables, or emptying the three big trash bins and lining up the bags at the back, where someone bigger than me will toss them into the Dumpster. I take my breaks when Rosalyn tells me to, sit with one or two of the others around a table in the back, and work on my invisibility skill. Maybe someday it will work; maybe someday I will shimmer away and disappear and be safe.

I'm almost at the end of my shift when it happens.

I'm in the inner corner of the café, my favorite place because it's secluded and few people choose to sit there. When they do, it gives me a place all to myself while I clean up after them. I feel safe, even start humming to myself as I make sure for the second time that every square inch of the tabletop is sparkling clean, but suddenly, when I turn around, a man is standing there, staring at me.

I straighten up slowly, slide behind my cart, my shield,

start pushing past him, but he doesn't budge, blocking my way.

"Excuse me," I mutter, inching the cart past him. It brushes against him, and he grabs the side of the cart, where my cleaning sprays sway back and forth, wraps his hand around the bar between the spray I use on the glass tabletops and the one I use on the wooden counters. "Wait," he says. "Wait a minute."

I glance at him, then away. He's not all that old, but a faint smell of pipe tobacco drifts from him, and that always reminds me of old men. His hair is black, starting to gray, his eyes sky blue, his face flushed. His shirt is white, his tie blue and gray. He looks normal, like any of the many men who drink their coffee here every day.

"I need to go . . . the waitress will help you," I say.

"Wait. I . . . I know you," he says.

I meet his eyes for a second before I recoil and my heart starts thudding, first slow but heavy, then faster but still heavy, like jungle drums inside my chest.

I know him, too.

I've never seen him before. But this has happened in a dream, over and over again, for years and years and years. In my dream I'm in a zoo, inside an enclosure, wearing dirty overalls and carrying a huge bucket filled with fragrant fruit. I'm feeding the elephants, and I feel small among the giants, tiny but still important, so important and so happy when the gentle creatures reach toward me with their trunks, accepting apples from my hand, nodding their huge heads in thanks as they toss the apples into their mouths.

Around us, on the other side of a brick wall, a crowd, people staring at me, at my elephants, but I don't mind. I'm proud of them, I'm proud of myself, and when a little kid atop his mother's shoulders waves, I smile and wave back.

Then a cloud passes in front of the sun, dimming the image of the elephants, the little boy, and when it's gone, all I see is a man. He's standing there in the crowd, a stranger whose face I never remember, and when he catches my eye, he smiles, leans over the wall, and gestures for me to step closer. My legs move, nothing I can do to stop it, and then I'm standing at the wall, my hands against the rough bricks, my arms straight, my muscles straining as I push against the wall to avoid being pulled even closer.

The man leans toward me, his hands resting on top of the wall, and I try to push backward, but I can't. The man smiles. He opens his mouth. I hear no sound, but his lips move and I see what he says, and there's something inside my chest, razor claws digging into my insides and shredding them.

I know you. The words are dark, dim, heavy. *I know you. I remember you.*

Behind me, a gray mountain roars and the world shakes as the elephant stands on her hind legs. The man lets go of the wall, and his gaze pulls off me and to the elephant above. His eyes widen as the sun is blocked, and then he's gone, trampled and vanished under the elephant's giant foot. A hole in the universe has opened and closed. And I'm safe. I'm free. I lean against the thick rough hide and wrap my arms around the huge leg, and the elephant touches my face with her trunk, strokes my cheek, wraps around my head with a tender pat, rubs up and down my back, and I'm safe.

I'm standing with a mop in my hand and looking into the eyes of a man who says he knows me.

The dream makes this familiar, and for a moment I feel secure, like it's a movie I've seen a million times before. I reach back with my hand, but there's nothing there. My palm doesn't connect with the rough hide of an elephant's leg, and the man still stands there.

He smiles nervously. Looks me up and down. "You're older, of course, but not that different." His eyes move down to my chest, to my name badge, lopsided on top of the Dungeon Café logo on my apron. His lips move slowly; I see them form my name. He smiles wider as he looks back into my eyes. He looks bigger. "I've often wondered about your name."

The freezer behind me hiccups, starts humming

louder. There's a strange pattern to the humming, and I look down at the tiled floor, see the same pattern—the tiles are vibrating. The whole world's humming, screeching, but it's not an elephant's roar.

"Go away. Leave me alone." The voice doesn't sound like mine, but it can't be anyone else.

"You don't understand. I mean no harm. I just . . . I know you. I've been thinking about you, all these years. I saw you here yesterday, and I went home and checked to make sure. I brought a picture. See. Look!"

Something is in his hands. He flips his wallet open, pulls something out. "Look!" he insists when I avert my eyes, and I obey—for a split second I look. It's a portrait of me, a circle cut out of an online picture printed on good-quality photo paper. It's cut carefully in a perfect circle. I'm ten years old. I know that from the kitten charm hanging on a chain around my neck. Mom gave it to me for my birthday, but the chain broke and I lost it before Christmas that year.

"You haven't changed much," the man says, smiling. "Most kids change so much when they grow older. I'm so glad you're still you."

"Leave me alone," I whisper, but this time I don't hear any voice and I don't think he does either.

"You're special," the man says. He slides the picture back into the thin wallet behind a credit card. "I always knew you were special. I always keep my eyes open, everywhere I go, in case I recognize someone, but I never thought I'd actually find you."

"What's going on?" Rosalyn is there. She has been watching, looking out for me like she always does, almost like a friend. She pushes me to the side, puts her arm over my shoulder and I stand still, try to imagine she's an elephant. "Sir, can I help you?"

The man says something, starts stuttering, then backs away, sits down, and mutters something about coffee.

"Sure, I'll bring you coffee right away."

Rosalyn tries to pull me with her and I want to follow, but my feet are frozen to the newly mopped tiles, and Rosalyn shrugs and lets go of me. She returns to the counter and coffeemaker. The man is sitting at a table, between me and Rosalyn. I can't move. I can't move past him. The man looks at me, his face even redder now. He glances around, stands up, walks toward the exit. Rosalyn looks up from the coffeemaker, calls after him.

"Sir? Your coffee?"

The man picks up speed. He's practically running when he reaches the exit.

Rosalyn rushes back to me. "What was that all about?" she asks. "Do you know that guy?"

I shake my head, feel Rosalyn's hand on my arm, shake her off, feel her concerned gaze on my face and hate it.

"What did he say to you? Are you okay? You look like hell."

My muscles spasm. Paralyzed one second, hyperactive the other. The mop clangs against the floor. The few people in the café turn around and look, stare at me, but I don't care. I pull the apron over my head, drop it to the floor. I run into the back and open the door. Rosalyn's behind me—she's calling something.

The bike's lock takes too long to open. I leap over the low fence and run.

CHAPTER THREE

My cell phone starts chirping when I've crossed a block or two. I yank it out of my pocket, see Rosalyn's number, and throw the phone into an alley, where it bounces off a Dumpster. I run faster. The skin on my back itches, like a centipede is crawling up and down. I feel like someone's behind me, following me, looking at me. I feel his eyes on my neck, but I never see anyone when I look back.

At first I'm aiming for home, but then I realize that he can find me, and I swerve into the first road I find, leading in a totally different direction. He saw my name tag. He spoke my name. He can ask around, find out where I live, come to my door.

I go to the mall, force myself to wander around for a while. I dodge the shop assistants and hide behind clothes or books or DVDs in one store after another until the shop detectives start looking at me funny. I don't see anyone anywhere, but that doesn't mean they're not there.

I sneak into the bookstore one more time, detour through teen fiction to the nonfiction section, and trail my finger along the shelves until I come to the green corner with all the animal books. On the bottom shelf there are fish and whale books. Above them, farm animals and pets, horses, cats, goldfish. At the top, birds. And below the birds, all the typical zoo animals: tigers and bears and lions and zebras and giraffes.

Elephants.

There is only one place where I can be safe.

I run out of the bookstore and out of the mall. The ATM at the bus station spits my money out, and then I'm on the bus, my forehead against the cool glass, looking, looking, looking, but nobody's following me. Not that I can see.

I shiver during the long bus ride out of town. The bus is half-empty. I keep counting heads, glancing at faces, wondering if someone is there, hiding behind one of the seats, following me, looking at me. I keep my hands on my knees, ready to bolt.

Nobody seems to be staring at me. They look out the window, or rest their heads back, napping or listening to music, but I can't be sure they're not looking at me.

Finally, I'm there. I wait until everyone else has stood and moved to the front of the bus and then I leave, holding on to the seats on both sides as I wait for an old man to hobble toward the exit. There could be someone behind me, someone lurking between the seats, and now

I'm an easy target, one at the end of the line. I look back. Forward. Take a step. Look back.

At my destination, a line. Tourists and children, lots of children with their parents. I hate lines. I try to pick the shortest one, behind a man pushing a three-year-old girl in a stroller. Behind me, a couple with two boys arguing about what to see first. The woman with the little girl steps back, pushing me into the boy standing half an inch behind me. I grit my teeth at her apology, don't turn around when the little boy complains. Oxygen sticks in my throat. Almost there. I'm almost there.

I push my money over the counter, and a smiling girl hands me an orange-and-green ticket and a map. I push through the turnstile, run, run, run through twisted paths, past laughing children and camera-clad tourists, until I'm there.

The elephant habitat is almost like my dream. It's barricaded with thick short cement walls, and above that, wire netting. I lean against the concrete wall, push my body against it, and stretch my hands out over it, stare at the elephants, small in the distance, but close enough. I breathe, breathe, feeling safer now, feeling merely lost instead of hunted.

I stand in the same spot for an hour, hook my fingers into a wire diamond, and push close, so that I can watch the elephants without seeing the wire, too. They're not close. They can't come close, not close enough to trample anyone. There's a no-man's-land between the barrier and the elephants, a low stubby wall. I guess elephants don't jump.

There are five elephants. One male and three females and one baby. I stare at the baby, playing with water and sand, hopping from one adult to another, getting loving attention everywhere. I envy her. They're all looking after her. She's safe.

My shoulders sink slowly, my jaw unclenches.

She's safe here. And so am I.

I wander around the zoo all day, getting to know the different paths, the different zones, but always returning to the elephant area. I don't know what to do, where to go. Every time I get close to an exit, his voice whispers inside my head. *I know you.* The smell of pipe tobacco drifts from the shark tank. *I remember you.* The smile, flashing on and off as I stare out into the parking lot on the other side of the exit; his eyes moving down to my name badge. His lips, forming my name. *I know you. I remember you.*

I can't go home. I can't go anywhere.

When it's feeding time at the elephant enclosure, I'm waiting, my hands clinging on to the netting as people start to gather. I'm at the front, with dozens of people crowding in on me, but it doesn't matter here.

A kid around my age walks toward the elephants, carrying a heavy bucket filled with fruit. His blond hair is long and shaggy; his T-shirt and baseball cap flash the orange-and-green zoo logo. The elephants look up. Their large heads turn toward him. The boy puts the bucket down. The elephants start walking, all of them, slowly making their way toward him, toward me. The baby runs, almost seems to skip. The boy says something to them, and they stop, forming a half circle facing us.

I hold my breath.

He's communicating with them. He's one of them.

This is what I want. This is what I need. I must get inside. Must get inside the circle of elephants.

I inch along the fence, trying to see the entrance into the elephant habitat. There are trees and bushes hiding any doors. Maybe I can hide somewhere, and after closing hours I can find a way inside.

"Why don't they step on him, Mommy?" a little girl asks.

"Because they like him, honey," her mother replies. "He's feeding them, look. Lots of yummy fruit."

"They're much bigger and stronger than he is. They could just step on him and take the bucket."

"Then he wouldn't be there tomorrow with a new bucket."

"Is that why they don't trample him?"

The mom sighs. "Maybe they like being nice and not hurting people, honey. You know, like we do."

When people start heading for the exits, I get scared. I wait for the closing announcement to echo over the zoo's speakers, and don't know what I'll do, where I'll go, how I'll make it through the night until the zoo opens again in the morning.

I'm not leaving. I can't leave.

I shuffle along random paths, trying to stay out of the way of the friendly zoo staff ushering people to the exits. I come to a place I noticed before, deep in the middle of the zoo, close to where the chimpanzees swing from their trees and make faces at the humans.

It's a cage. Not a big one. There's a sign with a lot of reading material, saying this cage held zoo animals once, before they got decent enclosures, a habitat, space to run and prowl. It says they keep the cage here to show people how zoo animals used to live, how they only had a couple of yards to walk back and forth.

Things have changed, but this is still a zoo—the cages are bigger and better and the walls cleverly hidden, but they're still cages. I guess in animal sanctuaries they could show pictures of zoos and talk about what horrible places they are, with the small habitats and bars and concrete and people staring and throwing popcorn and peanuts. And maybe in a hundred years they'll display a sanctuary, a fake prairie inside a circle of barbed wire and KEEP OFF signs, and show schoolchildren how appallingly we treated animals back then. It's a weird world when even right and wrong keep changing.

A large door at the side of the cage hangs open. A big sign encourages children to go inside and play, to imagine what life would be like locked in a small box for their entire life. Inside is a pile of hay. The cage is relatively secluded in a grove of tall trees, in between the chimpanzee zone and the gorilla zone. I look around, wait until nobody is in sight, and dash inside the open door. I throw myself into the hay, dry and brittle, littered with candy wrappers, sticky from the children's cotton candy. I dig myself in deep, and feel better.

I don't need to leave.

I'll be safe here tonight with the elephants close by.

I stay put until the closing announcements no longer whisper across the zoo. I wait, and the zoo gets quieter and quieter, and then louder, different noises, coming closer and closer.

The cleaning crew. Night guards too, probably.

I squeeze my eyes shut and clench my fists, feeling so stupid. The candy wrappers, empty paper cups. It's not safe here at all.

I sneak out of the cage, hide in the shrubs on the

opposite side, my back against a rough concrete wall. I know there are apes on the other side of that wall. I watch my cage through a tent of leaves, watch two men in green overalls arrive. They empty the cage of the dirty pile of hay and litter, hose down the floor, toss in piles of fresh hay, chat lazily about a movie they've seen. They move on, and I wait.

I wait until there are no sounds close by, until it looks like the cleaning crew has left because most of the lights along the paths turn off. And then I return to the cage.

I lie down in the fragrant fresh hay and feel happy, as if someone made my bed with clean linen, dried outdoors in the summer sun like my mom used to do. I stare up at the dark ceiling and smile. There are probably bugs scuttling all over me, spiders spinning webs along the ceiling, but I don't care.

In the distance owls hoot, and in reply there's a howl. The wolves? There are all kinds of strange sounds, all around me, but they are not frightening.

I prowl on my hands and feet through the sea of hay, like a lazy tiger, to the door, pull it shut. It squeaks, and as soon as I let go, it swings open again. If I could find a rope or a piece of string, I could tie the door shut and be safe inside, but I suppose someone could easily cut the rope from outside. I examine the door with my hands, almost blind in the darkness, and find a keyhole but no key.

It doesn't matter. This has to be good enough. I think about my bed at home. Unmade. My mess of a room. The open closets, the books in a messy pile on the shelves. Brian, in his room, or out in the garage, his music bombing through the walls, his screams when I play my own music on top. Aunt Phoebe, in her room in front of her television, the volume turned up as Brian and I start fighting.

I wonder what they're doing now. I wonder if they've called the police yet, or if Aunt Phoebe has called Mrs. Foster. I wonder if Brian cares at all that I'm gone.

I turn on my back; hay crackles around my feet as I twist my body around.

I wonder if the elephants sleep standing up, or if they lie down together in a pile of hay, like I do. I wonder if they huddle up around the baby and lay their trunks protectively over her back. I wonder if they snore.

I smile.

And I fall asleep.

CHAPTER FOUR

I awaken several times during the night, but only for a moment, only to blink into the darkness, squirm into a more comfortable position and fall asleep again. I sleep better than in my bed at home. The hay does something to me, the warm itchy hay and the cage with its bars. I feel like an animal, a burrowing animal running on instincts, a creature who wants nothing but a place to sleep, a long, safe, dark sleep.

Then suddenly it's morning. Before I open my eyes, I know something's wrong.

I've overslept. And someone's close by, whispering.

My muscles tense as my brain starts branching off a whole slew of what-if scenarios.

I open my eyes and see straw. I've sunk deep into the hay in my sleep. Through the straw I see a row of serious first graders lining up outside my cage, hands clutching the bars, their teacher behind them with a puzzled look.

"What animal is that, Miss Taylor?" one of the kids asks.

"It looks human," another one says, "but it's in a cage, so it must be an animal."

"Maybe this is the missing link," a third one adds authoritatively.

"Kids!" their teacher says. "Don't be silly. She's a person. She probably works here at the zoo." She looks closer. "Or perhaps her parents do." She smiles. "Hello."

I mutter something, feel them watching me as I crawl out of the straw, blinking dust out of my eyes. I leave the cage and walk away until I'm around a corner, then sprint to one of the public toilets. It's empty and clean, smelling of pine and citrus cleaner. I see a shadow in the mirror as I wash my hands—there's probably straw in my hair. I defocus my eyes until everything is blurry and look up into the mirror, run my hands through my hair until it seems to be less of a mess. The elastic that held back my ponytail is missing. It's somewhere in my cage, probably. I need to get up earlier tomorrow; I can't be still asleep when people arrive.

I feel filthy, but I can't do much about that. I didn't bring a change of clothes—I didn't bring anything. The money I withdrew from that ATM won't last forever, and there's not a lot I can buy without leaving the zoo. Only some food and whatever they have in the souvenir shop.

I imagine walking out the gates and feel empty.

I curl my hands, and my palms ache.

I don't even have my box.

Last year there was a picture of a needle in my biology

textbook. A microscopic image, magnified, impossible to miss when I flipped through the book the first day of school. A colony of orange bacteria crowded on the needlepoint. I'd never before realized there would be bacteria on needles, and the image made me so sick I had to run to the bathroom and throw up.

I had seven needles then, rolling loose in my nightstand drawer. When I'd finished throwing up, I went back to my room and dug them all out. I sat down at my desk, and the needles made a soft tinkling sound when they tumbled out of my palm onto a sheet of white lined paper.

I shuddered, thinking about the bacteria, but I pushed at them with my finger, slowly arranging the needles by the length and width of the needle. Some of them had dried blood on the points; some had tiny pieces of skin tissue stuck to them.

I got rubbing alcohol from the bathroom, and I scrubbed each one.

Ever since, I've had my tin box. It holds my needles in a proper needle container and a small bottle of disinfectant spray, a packet of sterile tissues, and balls of cotton.

I don't know how I'll manage without my box.

I put my hands behind my back and try to think of something else I'll miss from home.

Books. And music, too—lyrics. Words. I need words. Words to run through my brain, words from books, from music, from TV shows; lyrics, paragraphs, dialogue. The words march through my head one by one, fast and loud, blocking out the pictures in my head, the movies running in my brain. I need the words, drumming onward, obscuring the view, keeping me safe on the inside of my head.

Now I have no books, no music, and no needles.

Only the elephants. But they're enough. They have to be enough.

I wash the best I can with the nasty soap. Mom always said shampoo was overrated, but she would never have approved of me brushing my teeth with a finger.

I go back to the elephants, stand there most of the day. I lean against the concrete wall and stretch my hands toward the elephants grazing in the distance, imagine an invisible line arching from my fingertips, touching the elephants, linking me to them, linking us together for always.

Today is different. Yesterday I was visiting, but last night I moved in. Today this is my home, and I spend the day getting settled in, finding out where everything is and how to get there. I notice where people sit with their kids for lunch and sometimes leave whole meals behind practically untouched. I find out people often forget useful things in the bathroom. I try not to attract

attention, keep to the crowds, and try to keep track of
the staff, who is where, when. I search for possible hiding
places, entrances and exits, and when the zoo closes and
night falls, I know what to do and where to go.

The souvenir shop is close to the main entrance. I visit
when it's crowded, to avoid attracting the attention of
the people at the counter. I walk around it twice, making
note of everything I will be able to find there. I snatch a
toothbrush with a zebra pattern off the shelf and buy it
despite the ridiculous price. I make a note of shorts with
a tiger tail or peacock feathers on the bottom. They've
got loads of T-shirts, but the price is too high. Although
there is an ATM in the zoo, I can't use that one. If someone is looking for me, if Aunt Phoebe calls the police,
the ATM transaction would give my location away.

My second night in the tiger cage is not as restful as
the first one. I need a shower. I itch everywhere, and my
hair feels oily and disgusting and keeps falling in my face.
I dive into the hay, crawl around the bottom of the cage
like a blind fish exploring the bottom of the ocean, but
I don't find my elastic. Gone with the rest of the junk,
probably.

I sleep in fits, a few minutes at a time, until late in
the night—then I drop off, and again I oversleep, but
although my watch tells me the time is half an hour past
opening time, nobody's by my cage.

I go to the bathroom, brush straw from my hair with my hands, wash my hands and face, and since nobody's there, quickly try to wash my hair with the soap provided. It takes too long. It takes forever to get the soap out, and I start to panic—someone's going to walk in, see me washing my hair, guess that I have no business staying here, call security. I'll get thrown out, and they'll never let me in again.

But nobody comes. My hair is relatively clean, and my shoulders are soaked, but I feel much better. I blink at the mirror, notice my wet lashes before I defocus my eyes, and concentrate on combing my hair with my fingers until my blurry image looks almost normal.

I go sit on a bench, letting the sun dry my hair, and wonder what to do about breakfast. Mom used to say breakfast was the most important meal of the day, and she would not have approved of my leftover chocolate bar. Even one with peanuts, which technically is fruit.

"Hey!"

I twist around, see someone standing on the path. I clench my fists, open them, raise a hand in a halfhearted greeting as I prepare to scuttle away. It's the guy from the elephant arena. I've watched him two days in a row now, watched him feed the elephants, talk to them, play with them. I've sent waves of envious energy toward him, but I've faded into the crowd, and fortunately, he's never noticed. He's wearing the same zoo uniform—green trousers, orange-and-green T-shirt, and baseball cap that says PILGRIM'S ZOO over his blond hair, and I sigh as I back away, wishing I were the one who could walk into the elephant enclosure as if I belonged.

He walks closer, stops a few feet away. I stare at his feet and wonder if I can get away with bolting instead of waiting to see what he has to say.

"What are you doing here?" he says.

"I'm just . . . visiting," I say. "With my parents."

He takes a couple of steps closer, and I back away. "Really?"

"Yeah." I dig in my pocket, wondering if my ticket is still there, and if a ticket from two days ago will pass. "My ticket is here somewhere if you need to see it . . ."

"Where are your parents, then?"

I gesture vaguely. "Around here somewhere. I think they went to see the penguins."

He makes a sound—I think he chuckles. "Today is Monday. We don't open until two o'clock today."

My heart shrivels up. I duck my head, turn, and take a few steps away from him, but he moves, and is again standing in my way. I feel his eyes on me, curious, wary. "How did you get in here?"

I shrug.

"Have you been here since yesterday?"

I shrug.

"You don't like talking, do you?"

I shake my head.

I think he grins. "No problem." He gestures around. "Most of my friends around here don't talk much either."

He's wrong. The elephants are vocal. They make different sounds, and they have a special one when he enters their yard, welcoming him. I heard them yesterday and the day before as I stood by the netting, envy writhing inside me as he talked to them.

"You really shouldn't be here," he says. "There are rules and stuff."

"Sorry," I mumble, and start walking away. "I'm leaving."

"Where are you going? The gates are all locked. You can't get out without a key."

I stop. Because it makes no sense to run. He'd simply call a security guard to find me.

"Can you let me out?" I ask when he just stands and stares.

"Are you homeless?" he asks back. "A runaway or something?"

"Something." I start walking down the narrow path alongside the aquarium wall.

He's following me. "How come? You're only a kid."

"I'm older than I look."

"Still. How does someone like you become homeless?"

I shrug.

"Are you hungry? You can have some of the fruit if you want. It's for the chimps, but I'm sure they can spare some for a fellow hungry primate." He sits down in the grass, next to the DO NOT WALK ON THE GRASS sign, and grabs an apple from his pail, takes a bite. "Go on. Have some fruit."

I'm starving. I've been saving my money because I need to make it last, and I've hardly eaten anything in two days. Just some popcorn from an untouched box a little kid left on a bench, some French fries a woman didn't want, and ice cream from a vending machine. I'm picky and only eat leftovers if they haven't been touched, but I suppose long enough in here and I'll be gobbling down half-eaten sandwiches.

I reach into his pail, grab two bananas and an apple, and cautiously sit down on the other side of the bucket, ready to stand up in a flash. He's too friendly. There must be a catch.

"Have you been sleeping here?" he asks between noisy bites of his apple.

"Yeah."

"How long?"

"Just last night," I lie.

"Why?"

He's looking at me, talking to me, but it's not as bad

as usual. Not in here, where I'm safe. "Are you going to turn me in?"

He shrugs. "I don't know yet. Why are you here?"

I shrug.

"What's your name?"

My tongue is stuck. There's no way I'm telling him my real name. I never want to hear my name again. It's poisoned now, ruined. I look up and away, and I see a big hairy face glare at us from the gorilla habitat. I remember Mom's favorite movie. "My name's Leia."

He grins, eyebrows raised, and I feel stupid. I stare past him, at a small tree, close enough to see his expressions without looking at him. "Leia? Like the princess?"

I nod.

His grin widens, turns into a laugh. "Your parents *Star Wars* nuts or something?"

"Something."

"I'm Kyle. My mom runs this place. So naturally her only child is consigned to manual labor."

"What do the elephants feel like?" I ask suddenly. It's missing from my dream. I'm not sure what it feels like when I reach back and touch the elephant's leg.

"What do you mean?"

"What do they feel like when you touch them? Is their skin warm or cold? Do you feel their pulse through their skin? Are they soft or hard?"

The questions don't surprise him, like he must have heard them a million times before. "Their skin's rough. Wrinkled. More so as they're older. It's very thick. They're warm to the touch."

"Are they dangerous?"

"Well, theoretically, yes. But not really. Not to us. We've never had a serious elephant accident at Pilgrim's Zoo. They can get angry if provoked, of course."

"And they roar," I whisper. "They stand on their hind legs and roar, and when they slam back down, the earth trembles."

Kyle peers at me. "You're weird."

I am. I'm different and weird and I always will be.

"What's it like being homeless?" he asks.

I shrug.

"Do you sleep on park benches? Or in a cardboard box? Or under a bridge?"

I'm feeling brave now, not scared like I'd be if I was at school and someone was talking to me. The elephants are close by. I feel protected. "No. I sleep in a zoo."

"Where exactly?"

"Doesn't matter."

Kyle laughs. "I know this zoo inside and out. I can easily find your hiding place if I bother looking."

I shrug. "Whatever."

Kyle bites a final chunk from his apple. "How does

someone become homeless? Did your parents throw you out?"

"I don't have parents."

"You're an orphan." It sounds old-fashioned and pathetic, and I grimace. "That's too bad," Kyle says. "I'm sorry. I mean, my parents split, and I hardly ever see my dad anymore, but I still know he's somewhere."

"It's okay."

"Why did you come to Pilgrim's?"

I finish my banana, drop the peel back in the bucket like Kyle did with his apple core, and start on the apple, still starving. Juice runs down my chin. I wipe it away with the back of my hand, and don't answer.

"Maybe we could make a deal."

I drop the rest of the apple, draw my knees up to my chest, get ready to run. "I doubt it."

"Wait. You would like to stay here. Right?"

"Yeah."

"I could use some help."

"What do you mean?"

"Mom's on my case. There was a small . . . problem. We had a fight, and well, she thinks as long as she keeps me occupied here, I won't get into trouble somewhere else."

"So?" I say cautiously.

"I've got a million chores, every damn day for the

entire summer. Running back and forth, cleaning up messes from animals and people both, sweeping the ground, bottle-feeding orangutans, moving chairs and tables back and forth . . ." He groans. "If you help me out with some of the most boring stuff, I won't turn you in, and you can stay here as long as it works."

I think about it. Picture myself walking around among the crowds, picking up litter and piling up folding chairs. It is a nice image. I would be a part of the zoo, invisible almost.

But it couldn't work. I shake my head. "People are going to notice me. The staff. Your mom and everybody. If I'm doing your work."

"That's exactly the point. They're supposed to notice," Kyle says. "It's the perfect plan. It will give you an excuse to be here, and my mom keeps saying she wants to get to know my friends, so she'll be happy too." He rolls his eyes. "Of course, what she really wants is to keep an eye on my friends so she can make sure I'm not in bad company." He looks me up and down. "And despite the homeless thing, you don't exactly look like bad company."

I feel my face warm. I stand up and start walking, fast. "Leave me alone!" I yell when he follows me.

"What's the problem? I thought you wanted to stay at Pilgrim's for a while!"

When something sounds too good to be true, it

always is, and when something sounds bad, it's always even worse. Kyle is just a kid in trouble with his mom. He can't help me.

"I can't. I can't meet people." I've given too much away. "I can't have people see me," I amend. "Someone might recognize me."

"Is your face on a milk carton?"

"No. I told you. No parents. Nobody cares where I am."

"Nobody will recognize you." He's right at my back. "I'll give you one of my Pilgrim's T-shirts and baseball cap. Nobody will see past the uniform. Don't you see how perfect this is for both of us? Mom will be off my case, and you can get to stay. You know, you won't get away with this any other way. The staff aren't that many. They'll notice you're always around. And if Mom sees someone like you and thinks you're my girlfriend, my life will get a lot easier—"

I stop so quickly Kyle walks into me, and my face flushes like a flood racing over my face. "Your girlfriend."

"Duh. Yeah. That's what we'll want her to think."

I stare at the zoo logo on his shirt, wondering how he could possibly want people thinking someone like me was his girlfriend.

"My devoted girlfriend," Kyle continues, "keeping me out of trouble. Perfect cover for you, perfect cover for me. My girlfriend, hosing down the elephants in the name of love."

"No, no way, I can't . . ." I draw in a deep breath, hold it. "Hosing down the . . . elephants?"

"It's play, mostly. For fun. We don't have a trunk, so we spray them with a hose. Dylan is the guy in charge— he supervises the elephants and all the bigger animals. But I get to do a lot of the fun stuff, and you can join in."

There's music, somewhere. Probably just inside my head, notes trilling together, tripping over themselves in excitement. "You mean, I would be helping you take care of the elephants? Not only picking up litter and sweeping the ground?"

He nods. "Sure. It's easy. They're not that dangerous if you're careful. They're—"

"Okay," I interrupt him, terrified now that he'll change his mind, that I'll miss this chance. It's too good to be true—I know it's too good to be true—but at the moment I don't care. "I'll do it. We have a deal."

Kyle grins. "Cool. Come on, I'll show you how to muck elephant poop."

"You'll find out that most of the zoo worker's job is shoveling shit," Kyle tells me as he removes heavy shovels from a storage closet. "When I was in kindergarten, I once brought different kinds of poop for show-and-tell."

He looks at something behind me and grins. "Hi, Dylan! This is Leia, my . . . friend."

"Hey," Dylan says. He looks big; that's all I notice when I glance at him and nod a greeting. "You got your friend a uniform?" he asks Kyle.

I stare down at the oversize zoo T-shirt Kyle found me, and I've pulled on over my own long-sleeved shirt. I hold out the edges so I can admire the upside-down zoo logo and the words PILGRIM'S ZOO in bright-orange letters. I can't believe I'm wearing one.

"Leia loves animals," Kyle says. "I told her she could help out." He holds his arms out. "I mean, if she actually wants to shovel animal excrement, who am I to deny her?"

Dylan shakes a finger at us. "As long as your mom agrees and as long as both of you follow the rules and always, always do as I say."

Kyle bows. "Always, Master Dylan. Always."

"Well, if you're going to make your lady work, here's the tool of the trade." Dylan tosses a shovel toward me, and I grab it, then follow Kyle along a narrow path toward the elephant zone. Dylan comes after us.

"Was your teacher impressed with your show-and-tell?" I ask. I don't remember much from when I was little, and the only thing I remember bringing to show-and-tell was a seashell my mom had collected when she was a kid. It wasn't very pretty in itself, but she told me there had been a pearl inside. There wasn't anymore.

"My teacher complained about a stink, even if all the containers were closed. But the other kids were impressed."

I smile, noticing the unfamiliar muscles move in my face. "Did you collect it yourself?"

"Yeah. Mom took me into the habitats, and I collected the specimens myself with a small green shovel and put them in petri dishes with lids."

"Sounds like fun."

"The animals all seemed bigger back then," Kyle says. "Everything in the zoo was bigger. All the animals seem smaller now. Except for the elephants. They're always huge." He pulls a key chain from his pocket and unlocks a small door, and we enter a dark stable. It stinks. Dylan comes through the door after us.

I follow Kyle until we're inside the large elephant arena. Kyle puts the fruit bucket down, and the elephants start approaching.

I back away as the elephants get closer. They seem bigger here than from the other side. Not as big as in my dream, but big and . . . not scary, but intimidating.

I back into something and jump. "Watch out!" Dylan says. "Careful. No sudden moves."

"Why?" I ask. "What could happen?"

"They're friendly," Kyle says. "Don't worry. Don't scare her, Dylan."

"Well, the two of you are my responsibility while you're in here. So, be very careful."

"Are they . . . dangerous?"

"Yes," Dylan says. "If they're angry or afraid, or by accident, if we're not careful enough."

"Stop scaring her!" Kyle says. "Leia, these guys are very friendly. They won't trample on you."

"Well, not unless you give them a reason," Dylan adds.

My legs are trembling a bit as I picture one of those giants sitting down on me, accidentally or not. "Give them a reason? What kind of a reason would they be looking for?"

"Don't worry. Here." Kyle tosses me an apple. "Give this to Calliope. She's the baby's mom. They're all protective of Leda, but you really want to get on Calliope's good side. She's very open to bribery."

I hold out the apple. It's like a dream when the giant animal approaches, reaches toward me with her trunk, softly takes the apple from my trembling hand, and pops it into her mouth. Then her trunk hovers in front of my face, asking for more, the large eyes beseeching me, staring into me until I want to build her an altar and pile a hundred apples on top. "Wow," I whisper as her trunk weaves around my wrist, searching for another apple. I have goose bumps all over my body. "Wow. Wow."

Dylan chuckles. "You'll be fine. She likes you, and the rest will follow. Just be careful, no sudden moves, no loud noises."

"Check their drinking water," Kyle calls from a few feet away. "Over there. Just check that it's clean and the drain is working."

Dylan moves away, but the baby follows me to the trough, dipping her trunk into the water. She's beautiful. I watch as she points the trunk into her mouth and squirts the water inside. It almost looks like she's laughing.

"Everything okay?" Kyle asks. He's pushing wheelbarrows.

"I thought elephants used their trunk to drink, like a straw."

"Nah," Kyle says. "That would be like us drinking through our noses. Which, while something I have attempted on occasion, I wouldn't recommend doing on a daily basis."

Oh. I have read a lot of books, but I bet there are still a million things I thought I knew but really don't.

"Okay, now we get to the fun part. Get your shovel. Use gloves. You'll need them or your hands will blister. Well, they'll probably blister anyway, but not as quickly."

Elephant poop is heavy and stinky, and there is a lot of it. We shovel it into the wheelbarrows and haul everything away to a manure Dumpster.

"Okay," Kyle says, tossing his gloves in a pile. "Now we sweep outside."

I follow him, looking over my shoulder back at the elephants. I pause as baby Leda reaches up to her mother with her trunk, and stop and turn around when Calliope lies down and rolls on her back in the sand.

"Come on," Kyle says, holding the door open.

"Wait," I say. I hold my breath while Calliope lumbers to her feet again.

"You're slowing me down," Kyle grumbles as he finally gets me out of the elephant habitat and locks the door behind me. "Tomorrow you'll be on your own for a lot of these chores. So pay attention."

"What are you doing tomorrow?"

"Hanging out with my friends," Kyle says. "Or, as Mom would say, keeping bad company. As long as my chores get done, and they see me every now and then, Mom and her fellow prison wardens will assume I'm somewhere around. They may ask you, and you'll tell them I'm around. I'll show up somewhere a couple of times and make sure someone sees me. As long as you keep your end of the bargain, it will work."

I picture myself lying to faceless people, answering

questions, blushing and stuttering like I always do. "What if they don't believe me?"

"You make them believe you. If you want to stay, that's what you do."

We move from one habitat to another—feeding, cleaning, playing with the animals—and in between there are floors to sweep and chairs to wipe down. There are no visitors, but there are people, staff, Kyle's friends. He introduces me as "my friend Leia," which makes me feel strange, but I manage to smile at people, and sometimes shake their hands. "She's a bit shy," Kyle mutters once or twice when people ask me something and I start to stutter. He glares at me, and I feel stupid and useless, but keeping Calliope and baby Leda in my mind helps.

I'm exhausted by the time Kyle announces his chores are done. "Time for a shower," he says. "Then I'm out of here for the day." He gestures to the administrative building. "Do you want me to show you where the women's showers are?"

I gape at him.

"What?" he asks.

"Did you say showers?" I ask, scratch my head where it itches, and nearly drool with joy.

"Believe me, you need one," Kyle says. I almost skip

after him into the building. He vanishes through one
door after pointing out another one to me. The doors
have the typical male and female signs on them.

It is the promised land. A real shower with a lock on
the door, soap and shampoo, and a pile of towels. Warm
water. I shower with my eyes closed and realize Mom
was so wrong about shampoo being overrated.

With reluctance I pull my old clothes on again and
decide to splurge on a T-shirt and shorts at the souvenir
shop. At this point I'd rather be hungry than dirty.

It's not easy to decide whose tail I want on my shorts,
but the shirt I grab in an instant: a gray one with the
profile of an elephant's head on the front. One large eye
stares out from my collarbone, and the trunk hangs down
to my hip. One ivory tusk crosses my front like a sword.

I leave the souvenir shop, put on my new clothes in
the restroom, and wash my old ones in the sink, wondering where I can leave them to dry. For now I put them in
the bag my new clothes came in.

By habit I shuffle back in the direction of my cage,
like I'm going home, but the zoo has opened now, and
my cage is occupied. I sit on a bench outside and stare
at the children playing in the hay, in my bed, and I think
about the elephants, the trunk on my hand, the large
legs, the dark tough hide, the intelligence in their eyes,
the soft bleating as Calliope calls baby Leda to her side.

I close my eyes and imagine myself tottering around the elephant enclosure. I wish I could sleep inside. I wish I could curl up underneath an elephant, between the four giant legs, with the comforting belly a canopy above me. I feel like I could sleep there forever, a deep dark refreshing sleep with the elephant guarding over me. I wish I were Leda, not a fake Leia.

CHAPTER   FIVE

I wake up on time the next day, my heart pounding as soon as I open my eyes, but from excitement, not fear. I clean up my cage, then myself, pull on the zoo T-shirt, and sit on the bench closest to my cage, waiting for Kyle.

An eternity later, he's finally there, his hair still mussed from sleep, yawning. He sits down next to me and rubs his eyes. "I can't believe Mom drags me down here every morning at eight o'clock," he groans. "It's summer! This is practically child abuse!"

"Where are we going first?" I ask when he looks like he's going to start snoring.

"Kyle! There you are." A blond woman wearing a uniform and sunglasses walks toward us. I can tell from her hair she's Kyle's mom. I make an extra effort to seem normal when Kyle introduces me as: "Leia. A friend. She's helping me out with all the million chores you saddled me with."

Eve removes her sunglasses, shakes my hand warmly, and smiles.

"I love to meet Kyle's friends," she says. "Glad to hear

you like the zoo. Not everybody does when they're not little kids anymore. Some people think it's too smelly and dirty and noisy."

"She's talking about my dad," Kyle stage-whispers. "He used to be comanager here, but then he dumped both us and the zoo for a brunette with a law degree."

A shadow crosses Eve's face. "Kyle . . . ," she says with a sigh, and for a moment I wonder why he's acting like this when she seems so nice. Then I remember things aren't always what they seem.

"Dylan told me you two were in the elephant habitat yesterday," she says. "Kyle, Dylan thought you had my permission. You did not. Leia, this is not your fault, but don't follow Kyle blindly. He has been known to walk into dead ends and get stuck there."

Kyle makes a disgusted sound. "Mom . . ."

Eve smiles. "I will need to talk to your parents in order to allow you access to the habitats, and then always under Dylan's strict supervision. Drop by my office when you like, and give me your parents' names and phone numbers."

"Right," I mumble, and want to glare at Kyle for getting us in trouble.

"It's great to have you around, Leia," Eve says. "But don't let Kyle bully you into doing his job for him."

"No," I say, "I'm not. Really. It's just . . . it's fun to help out a bit. I love animals."

Eve smiles at me and nods. She tries to sneak a kiss on Kyle's temple, but he jerks away. "I'll see you kids around," she says. "Be careful."

"Nice," Kyle says with a hint of surprise when his mother is out of earshot. "She likes you. Good job."

"Why are you so mean to her?" I ask.

"I'm not mean to her."

I shrug. It's none of my business.

Kyle stands up. "Okay. Let's get started. I'll deal with the apes. You handle the elephants. Muck and feed. Not necessarily in that order. Then . . . I don't know after then. I can't think this early in the morning. We'll see."

"The elephants? By myself? Didn't you hear what your mom said?"

He yawns. "I heard. I know Mom's schedule. She goes straight to a meeting—she'll be tied up until noon. Dylan will be there too. So nobody's going to notice."

I picture myself against the wall in the elephant enclosure, with the big male approaching. "Your mom is not the giant wild animal I was worrying about."

Kyle shrugs. "What's to worry about? Any trouble, you just leave. Any questions, come to the ape habitat and get me. I'm easy to find—I'll be the least hairy ape around."

"But what if I do something wrong and they sit on me or something. . . . What if—"

Kyle rubs his eyes. "You did fine yesterday. You took forever, but it was fine. The elephants loved you, and you know elephants never forget. Do you want this job or not?"

"The pay is lousy," I mutter.

"Quit complaining. You're getting room and board," Kyle says. He pushes himself to his feet and heads for the food storage with me in tow. "What do you want for breakfast, banana or watermelon?"

Kyle slices up some watermelons while I eat a banana and a kiwi. "The elephants love watermelon," he says, loading my cart with a ton of fruit and grain. "It's their favorite. So, give them some, and they'll love you forever."

"Gee. Maybe they'll trample all over me in excitement."

"Here, keys." He hands me a key chain, two keys hanging from a small metal elephant. "I lost mine once but found them again, so now I have two sets. The larger key works on most of the bigger doors, the smaller one on regular doors. That's the general rule, anyway. They work on the habitats and cages but not on any buildings. If there's a door you can't open with these two, you're not supposed to go there."

"You mean, *you're* not supposed to go there. I'm not supposed to go anywhere."

Kyle doesn't listen. "If anyone asks questions, you tell them you're with me."

"Right. And then when your mom finds out, she's going to pick a cage and throw us inside for good."

Kyle takes a deep breath. "Well, if you'd rather call your parents and get permission . . ."

I shake my head.

"Fine, then. When you're done, come back to me. You should be finished long before I am."

"Okay."

I push my cart toward the elephant area, nervous and excited both at once. Being with the elephants was magical, but being alone with them will be unbelievable. I glance around before I unlock the door, and rush inside, relieved not to see anyone.

Kyle is right. The elephants love watermelon. I end up hiding the watermelon at the bottom of the cart, so the elephants will take some of the other fruit and grain too. "It's dessert!" I tell Leda as she tries to sneak her trunk toward a melon, and gently push her head away with a nervous glance at her mothers and aunties, not sure they approve of me teaching Leda table manners. "Now, first an apple. And some grain. Grain is good for your digestion."

I stay for a while, patting the elephants, playing with them like I watched Kyle do yesterday. Someone passes by, but she raises a hand in greeting, accepting that I belong there, and I wave back, feeling secure and confident in my zoo T-shirt, with the elephants by my side.

Then I reluctantly leave the habitat and trudge back toward the primate area to search for Kyle. I find him with the orangutans. He has a baby wrapped around his neck, and the mother eating out of his palm, and he doesn't look all that miserable to be stuck doing zoo chores.

"You missed the fun stuff," Kyle says when he sees me. "Playtime's over." He untangles himself from the baby's long arms and pushes him back to his mother, and we start mucking.

Smells flare up when we stick our shovels under the scattered messes, and I wrinkle my nose. "If apes are so smart, why don't you toilet train them?"

"Not a bad idea," Kyle says.

I'm sweaty and dirty when we're done, but it doesn't matter anymore because I know I can get a shower.

We leave the orangutans and return the carts to the storage. Kyle gets us bottled water from a fridge, and we sit down in the grass, next to another DO NOT WALK ON THE GRASS sign, the chilled drink a welcome change from the tepid tap water I'm used to.

I flinch when he reaches out, but he doesn't touch me, just gestures to a straw I hadn't realized was stuck in my hair. He grins. "I figured it out. You sleep in the old tiger's cage, don't you? The one we keep for the kids to play in?"

I glare his way. "Well, I used to."

He looks at me with pity. "Can't be fun. I can probably get you a key to the basement of the administrative building. It's separated from the rest of the building, just one giant room for storage. No security system, nobody ever goes there, nothing there but junk and mice. But better than a cage."

I shake my head. "No, thanks. I'm fine."

"You'd rather sleep in a cage that's on display for not being suitable for animals?"

"Yeah."

"You've got to be kidding . . . oh . . . you've got that thing."

"What thing?"

Kyle's brow furrows. "I saw a documentary. Some mental disease. Some kind of a phobia. They said some homeless people were homeless because being inside buildings terrified them. Is that what's wrong with you? Is that why you're homeless? And the cage is okay because you can see out?"

I shrug. "Don't worry about me."

"Can't they cure whatever is wrong with you? A pill or something? Don't they have a pill for everything?"

I want to tell him nothing is wrong with me, but I can't. There is something wrong with me, but I don't know what it is or what it's called or how to fix it. I only know that I'm broken.

"Maybe I don't want a pill."

"I bet my mom knows a shrink who can help you. Maybe hypnosis or something. You could ask her. Or I could ask her for you, I suppose."

"I'm fine! Stop trying to figure me out!"

"Okay. I was only trying to help."

I think about my cage, my home. "If you really want to help, there is one thing you can do for me."

"What is it?"

I hold my key chain up, my fingers securely around the elephant's middle, the two keys dangling from its trunk. "You can get me the key to my own cage."

Kyle shrugs. "I'm not sure there even is a key to that thing."

"There is a keyhole. There must be a key."

"The cage is a hundred years old—what are the odds of the key lying around somewhere?"

He stands up, chucks the empty bottle into a recycling bin. "Come on. I want to show you something."

He takes me through a storage building filled with boxes, and to the other side, through a door marked QUARANTINE, until we're standing by another set of bars.

On the other side is a small habitat, isolated, closed off
from the public, an outdoor area closed off by buildings
on all sides. It's got grass and trees, and ropes hanging
from tree to tree. At first I think it's empty, then I see a
tiny movement.

It's a small ape, skinny, with a narrow, worried face
and big eyes. She sits in the shadow of a tree, not moving.
I grab the bars with my hands and press my face between
them to see better.

"Her name is Tina," Kyle says. "She arrived yesterday.
She's a chimp, probably around five years old."

"What's wrong with her? Why is she in quarantine?
She looks really sick."

"No, she's not sick. Not in that way. She just needs
peace and privacy."

"Why?"

"She was rescued by Animal Welfare. We don't know
what happened to her, but she's got scars all over under
her fur."

Pain claws over my insides. I hear the sounds of anger,
fury, a sadistic chuckle. I feel a belt. An iron bar. A two-
by-four. Slashing the air, striking my back. I feel a fist in
my stomach, a heavy boot on my fingers. I feel random
thoughts on a collision course: run, hide, fight, surrender.
Bad, worse, worst, everywhere. No safe place, no safe
people.

"She's very traumatized," Kyle continues. "She behaves nothing at all like our regular chimpanzees. She's almost like another species."

I hunch down, staring into the habitat, push my arms through the fence, and reach toward her, but she's far away. Tina's eyes are large and brown, her brows heavy, and she's more still than any creature should be. She stares at my hands, and I withdraw them when I sense her fear. She doesn't know she's safe now, doesn't know my hands won't hurt her, doesn't know all I want is to heal her. She looks damaged, even though her scars aren't visible under her fur; the wound is inside her mind, and her eyes tell me the whole story. *I'm broken*, I can almost hear her whisper. *Please, fix me.*

"Can you help her?" I whisper.

"Mom's trying. She's contacting some experts. But there's not much we can do here. We can provide her with shelter and safety, not much else. This is temporary. They're trying to find a sanctuary to take her in."

Tina lets out a low wail. I straighten up, and breath is forced from my lungs in a rush of fury. "Why? I don't understand. Why would someone beat her?"

"It happens quite a lot. An easy way to train chimps is by using fear."

"They hurt her because it's *easy*?"

Kyle shrugs. "People do all kinds of bad things for no

good reason at all. Would it make a difference if they had a good reason? What would be a good reason anyway?"

Tina looks so alone. Again I reach through the bars toward her, but even though she is at a safe distance, she cringes and pulls away.

"Why can't you put her with the other chimps? Will she attack them?"

"She might. Or be attacked," Kyle says. "That's just as likely. Animals often don't show a lot of tolerance for someone who's different. Plus, she doesn't belong in a zoo. Our chimps are used to being here—they even like the attention—but this one wouldn't be able to handle the crowd. She needs a sanctuary."

"But in a sanctuary she would need to be around other chimps. Right?"

Kyle nods. "Yeah."

"Will she be able to do that?"

"I don't know. They'll try to train her. Teach her to be a normal chimp. I don't know if it's possible. She sure is nothing like a normal chimp now."

Tina moves, rocks forward and back. A sighing sound skims off her. I stare, and she seems to notice. Her shoulders hunch; the rocking intensifies. I know what she feels; I know my gaze is like a million needles boring into her; I know how much it hurts, and I look away. I look at Kyle instead—for a moment I look into his eyes, then past him, over his shoulder when he looks back at me. His eyes are brown. I'm glad I know that now.

"Why does she do that?" I ask through the lump in my throat. "Why does she rock back and forth like that?"

Kyle pushes his hair away from his face. He's staring at Tina with a frown. "It's what chimps do when they've suffered a lot. Many species do something like this. Humans, too, Mom says."

"Can't we help her? Can't we do something? She's sitting there alone and scared—can't we do something for her?"

Kyle shakes his head. "There's not much we can do. A zoo is no place for a traumatized animal. Until she gets to a sanctuary, all we can do is give her a safe space, and hope she figures out that nothing bad is going to happen to her anymore. That's all we can do, try to show her this isn't a bad place. But she has to discover it on her own."

"Maybe this is hopeless," I whisper.

"Not necessarily. The sanctuaries have experts who deal with stuff like this. They can help her."

"I don't know. How can she ever feel safe? I mean, she knows what can happen. She knows what people are capable of. So she knows it can happen again. It doesn't matter how often everybody's nice to her—she knows evil is out there too, waiting."

"Maybe in time she'll forget."

"No."

"You don't think so?"

I shake my head, tears for Tina gathering behind my eyes, but I don't let them through. "She'll never forget. She can't forget. She has to be prepared in case it happens again."

CHAPTER SIX

After the chores I spend most of the day by Tina's habitat. Just before closing time Kyle meets me there and hands me something large and heavy wrapped in a hand towel.

The key is no ordinary key. It's like something out of a fairy tale or a computer game, something to open an intricate iron door to a dungeon or a castle tower. It's big, about the size of my hand, heavy, and red with rust. There's a sticker on it: "Old tiger cage" scrawled in green ballpoint.

"Thanks," I say, and Kyle shrugs.

"If you're caught, you didn't get the key from me," he says. "But nobody's been using that key for ages; they'll assume it got lost a long time ago."

I scratch the sticker off. "Right."

"What do you want it for? You can't lock the cage during the day—people will notice if the kids can't play inside anymore."

"Doesn't matter . . ." I clench my hand around the key, glance at my watch. I need to be alone. I need the day to be over.

Just in time, the closing announcement drifts over the zoo.

"Closing time," I say. "Don't you have a megaphone to chant into or something? Bad company to join?"

I feel guilty when he looks hurt and leaves, but I can't wait for the zoo to empty, can't wait to claim my home. I vanish into one of my hiding spots for the long wait, but when the staff has left, when the cleaning crew has left, the zoo's finally all mine. I get inside my cage, pull the door shut, and insert the key. Rust scrapes against rust; a red cloud shivers around the lock as I try to turn the key. But it works at last. Something clicks, and the door no longer moves. I put the key back in my pocket, grab the bars of the door, and shake it. It doesn't budge. I'm locked in.

"Hey, the key worked."

I step back from the bars as my heart starts to race, but it's only Kyle. He's been standing in the shadow of the trees on the other side of the path. He probably saw my hiding place too.

"You're spying on me."

"That cage is an exhibition. You're the one who locked the door and put yourself on display."

I fluff up my hay, pull my backpack and my water bottles within reach, and settle down, munching on an apple. "I don't care," I say between noisy bites, and realize that I don't. I'm in here, the key is in my pocket, and the cage is locked. "Gawk all you like."

Kyle steps closer. His hands curl around the bars, higher than the kids reach. A few flakes of rust fall down, settle on the fresh hay scattered around the bottom of the cage. "Maybe we need a new sign," he says. "Leia: homo sapiens weirdo. Age: teenage. Natural habitat: unknown. Feeds on chocolate and scavenges fruit from other ape species."

I scowl. "Whatever."

Kyle grins. He steps closer, pushes a paper bag between the bars. "I brought you a couple of books. Just animal stuff from Mom's office. In case you're bored. There's a flashlight, too. I put in fresh batteries."

Reading books by flashlight. I remember doing that when I was little, Mom catching me, trying not to smile as she took the flashlight away and told me to go to sleep.

I stare at the bag as it sinks into the hay, wondering why he's doing this.

Because everybody, always, has a hidden agenda.

I look at him, but his face tells me nothing.

"Thanks," I mumble, and he waves as he leaves.

By the time the sun rises the next morning, I've spent hours reading about evolution, and when the clock approaches opening time, I unlock the cage, swing the door open. The kids will play inside today, but tonight it will be mine again, a room of my own.

The days settle into a quiet, wonderful routine. I do Kyle's chores in the morning, spending as much time as I can with the elephants before the zoo opens, all the while trying to keep out of Dylan's way. After opening hours I stay with Tina as much as I can, sitting by the bars separating us, talking with her, singing to her, playing, or sneaking her food. Sometimes Kyle's there too. I'm not hungry anymore because I have a key to the fruit storage, and Tina and I share bananas and apples and watermelon.

Tina is family. Our closest relative among all the animals. But the elephants feel like family too. I'm one of them now. They know me. They like me. I'm still nervous when I enter their habitat, but never scared, just respectful enough to be careful. I'm nervous of them like I am nervous of cars aiming at me at full speed, or a piano dangling above my head. It's a natural, normal kind of fear, not a crazy fear.

"Elephants are related to us too," I say to Kyle one day. I run a finger along my own nose as I stare at Leda's little trunk, shoveling watermelon into her mouth. "Imagine, being related to elephants."

"Yeah. It's not so crazy. I mean, all living things on earth are related."

"How far back are we related to the elephants?"

"Do you expect me to remember stuff like that?" Kyle points. "There is a sign outside that will tell you. It's the small print in the corner."

I have read every sign in the zoo, but I don't remember the details. We check the sign on our way out. It says that the common ancestors of us and the elephants lived about a hundred million years ago. They were among the first placental animals, and looked a lot like shrews. Between them and us are forty-five million individuals. Forty-five million individuals have lived since my ancestor and Leda's ancestor were the same individual. That individual had two kinds of offspring—one of them led to elephants and the other to humans.

It's a crazy thought. Still, it means Leda is my cousin.

"You know about the evolutionary path you can take through the zoo, don't you?" Kyle asks.

I shake my head.

Kyle pulls a zoo map from his back pocket. It's a bigger version of the map every visitor gets when they enter the zoo. I've seen Kyle and the other staff members show this map to visitors when they ask something. "If you take this route from the Orange exit, you meet some of our most distant relatives first, then move closer and closer to our own lineage. Look, here, we have the primates. First you pass the monkeys, then the apes, then the great apes, our closest cousins. And here, at the very center of the zoo, guess what's here?"

I squint at the map, trying to fit the location he's pointing at to the map in my head, but give up. "I'm not sure. The gorillas?"

Kyle chuckles. "Close. No, this is your cage."

"My cage? The old tiger cage? How do tigers fit in with the primates?"

"Not the tigers. It's Mom's private joke. She knew kids would be in and out of that cage all day, so she put that in the center. An ongoing exhibition of the young of homo sapiens sapiens. We're just another animal, she says, so why not put us on display too?"

I trail a finger back along the path on the map, away from my cage, past the primates, past several mammal species, to the elephants.

"Being related to the elephants means we share genes with them."

"Yeah. Loads. Not that it means much. We also share loads of genes with rice and robins and roaches and roses and . . ." Kyle looks around, as if to look for more species starting with an *R*.

I look down at the rocky bed inside the barred elephant fence. "Rocks? It's too bad rocks don't have DNA. That would be cool. We could have diamond DNA . . ."

Kyle kicks a can in the direction of a bin. "Or metals. Aluminum DNA . . ."

"Yeah."

"Copper and tin would mate, and produce little bronze babies . . ."

"But why did your mom put us in the center?" I ask. "I mean, the homo sapiens' cage? Isn't it a bit conceited to have this path leading up to the human, like we're automatically the pinnacle of evolution?"

Kyle shrugs. "It's our zoo. If penguins had built this zoo, they'd have put themselves at the center, right?"

Tina has a fixed schedule for playtime, social interaction, and feedings, so usually I can make sure I come and go when no one else is there. But one day Kyle's mom stops by, smiles distractedly to me, and says hello, then stands by the bars for a while, looking at Tina. I back away to a corner, worried she will go inside the habitat, worried that she'll terrify Tina, but I'm being stupid. She's the expert, after all. She's the one who gave Tina shelter here in the first place.

"She's looking better, isn't she?" Eve says at last. "Her eyes are bright, and she's playing. She doesn't look terrified like she did all the time during her first days with us. And she's filling out. She actually looks quite healthy. Baby steps, but this is excellent progress in only a few days."

"Yeah," I say. I want to say something more, about how Tina sometimes asks me to play, or how she still doesn't dare take fruit out of my hand when I reach through the bars, but I'm not sure I'm supposed to spend so much time here, so I shut up. But Eve reads my mind.

"I know you've been spending a lot of time with Tina," she says. "Maybe we have you to thank for some of her progress."

I look down, mute.

"Where's Kyle?" she asks, looking around.

My heart beats faster. Kyle doesn't leave the zoo a lot, not nearly as much as I thought he would, but I hate being responsible for the excuses.

"I think he went back to the orangutans," I say, stammering a bit. "The baby really likes him. He sometimes has a bit of trouble getting away."

"You like him too, don't you?" she says, and my face turns redder than the apple in Tina's hand. "Sorry," she says, laughing. "I didn't mean to embarrass you. But you guys seem to be together all the time—you're always around here. So he must like you a lot."

I bite my lip and look down.

"I'm really glad he has such a close friend," Eve says. "He's had some problems lately."

"Bad company," I say automatically. Eve looks surprised.

"He told you about that?"

"Not exactly . . . ," I say. "I just . . . assumed."

She nods. "I think we're past that now. We have some trust issues. At the moment he resents me, but we will recover. And now with you in the picture, I think he'll be fine. You two are very different, but I think you ground him a bit. I'm glad he has you."

I look away. I'm such a total fraud.

"I'm sorry," Eve says. She laughs. "Now I'm really embarrassing you. You guys are just kids, and here I'm talking to you like you're my daughter-in-law."

I stare in utter absorption at the muddy floor.

Eve grins, she wiggles fingers at me as she leaves, and I sink down to an overturned crate and feel exhausted.

Tina comes closer after Eve leaves, sits down a few feet away from the bars, and starts rocking. She still sits and rocks back and forth a lot, but not as much as she used to.

I try something new. I inch closer to the barrier between us, cross my legs, and place my hands at each side of my head like Tina does. I hunch over and start rocking. It's strangely soothing, but I get bored quickly. So does Tina. She sits still, staring at me. I break eye contact and rip some grass from the ground on her side of the bars. I weave a long straw around my finger, wrap a blade of grass around my thumb. A tiny ant crawls over the back of my hand, climbs gratefully onto the familiar grass. I put my hand on the ground and allow the ant escape.

Tina sighs.

"Bored?" I ask her. She blinks.

"See what I've got?" I reach into my pocket, hold up a small orange plastic container, another treasure someone left behind at the zoo. Tina stares. Curiosity brings her a few steps closer; then she sinks to the ground and blinks some more.

I unscrew the lid, pull up the top. Put the plastic stick against the wires and blow. A long string of soap bubbles floats through the air toward Tina.

She stares, lumbers to her feet, goes cross-eyed when a large bubble comes closer and closer, sneezes in surprise when the bubble bursts against her nose. Then she starts the chase, hands and feet in a blur as she slams against every bubble she finds, and in a little while I'm lying on the ground, my stomach aching from too much laughter, and she still hasn't had enough. She holds out a hand, yapping at me. For once I understand chimpese: *More!*

My hands are wet and slippery, the cuffs of my shirt soaked. I turn the soap container upside down. Some froth leaks out, but that's all. "We're out of soap," I tell her. "I'll bring more tomorrow. Promise."

Tina sits down, crosses her arms, glares at me. I put

the soap container in my pocket and pull out a banana instead.

Bananas are still a favorite. I reach between the bars, holding a banana out. She looks at it, up at my eyes, and back down at the banana. Her mouth works. She makes a sound. She wants that banana, but she's still too afraid. She thinks the soap bubble game might be a trick. She thinks I may lash out. Maybe hit her with an iron bar, or kick her in the stomach, or pull her fur so hard it comes out.

I shudder. It hurts to imagine someone treated her that way.

I toss the banana her way. One hand shoots up and catches it. She peels her banana, smirking, like she outsmarted me.

"Nobody's going to hurt you anymore," I tell her for the hundredth time. "Don't worry, cousin. You're safe. The bad people are gone."

Her brows are heavy as she looks at me. I can almost hear her tell me that the bad people are never gone. She holds the banana peel upside down, high above her head, and looks inside.

"Eve's looking for a place for you. A sanctuary where there's peace and quiet and no sticky little yelling kids. You're going to love it. Eve's a good person. I know she'll do everything she can to help you."

Tina yawns. The banana peel flies through the air, lands in front of me on the other side of the bars. From ten feet away Tina holds out a hand. I look around to see if anyone's there, then reach inside my jacket and get the other banana.

"Don't tell anyone," I whisper as I toss the banana to her. "I'm not sure you're supposed to snack between meals. They have you on this super-balanced diet to make up for your malnutrition, and if you snack between meals, you may miss out on some of those carefully calculated calories."

Tina gobbles down the banana and holds out her hand again. I search my pockets, but all I have left is a chocolate bar. I hold out my hands and shrug, my all-out-of-food sign, and Tina makes a dissatisfied sound, leaps back, climbs into a tree, and glares at me.

"Sorry!" I call, settle back with my chocolate bar, and a soda can someone forgot to pick up from the vending machine yesterday. I'm almost out of money after buying the clothes at the souvenir shop. I try not to think too much about that. I can survive on fruit and food that people leave behind. I'll be fine.

Tina hears the rustle of the wrapper and jumps out of the tree, runs toward me. She stops a few feet away and holds out her hand, and when I don't oblige, she moves closer, her eyes insistent, determined, her sounds eager and impatient.

I tear the wrapper off the chocolate and break the bar in two. I put one half in my mouth, hold the other one out toward her through the bars. She reaches out, withdraws, backs off, then approaches again, the dance repeated again and again. The chocolate starts melting in my hand, but my perseverance pays off. In the end Tina reaches out, grabs the chocolate, and slumps away with a victorious shout.

For a second our hands touch.

I sit smiling with half a chocolate bar sticking from my mouth, and melted chocolate dribbling down my chin. On the other side of the fence Tina lies on her back, one arm under her head, sunning herself and grinning her way through her half of our chocolate.

Contact. We're sisters now.

CHAPTER SEVEN

One day I find a small hand mirror on the ledge below the large mirrors in my favorite restroom. I have a small pile of things hidden away in one of my secret hiding places, stuff people left behind or dropped to the ground, but I've never found a mirror before. There are giant mirrors in the public restrooms, but I can't look into them. They're too big and bright.

But I'm curious to look at myself, to see how I've changed.

I take the mirror outside; sit down at a secluded table in the picnic area. I pull my key chain from my pocket, hold on to the keys so that the heavy elephant charm faces downward. I bring my hand up, then slam it down onto the mirror.

At home I'd use a small hammer, but the elephant does the job. The mirror cracks, the fractures stretching out from the middle. I shake the mirror, but none of the pieces fall out of the frame, and I lift it up and look. This is the right way for me to look into the mirror. The only way. When it's broken too.

I look into one piece of the mirror at a time, breathing slowly, careful not to meet my own eyes. My hair is lighter from the sun. My face is tanned. My nose is sprinkled with freckles. I've changed. Maybe in time I can change enough for no one to recognize me. Maybe in time I can change so much I won't even recognize myself.

"Jeez, you're definitely not superstitious."

The mirror drops out of my hand. It falls onto the ground, and two pieces fall out, two jagged pieces of glass reflecting the green crown of the trees behind me. "Thanks!" I growl at Kyle, bending down to retrieve the mirror and the shards. "Now you've ruined it."

"Maybe I misunderstood something. Wasn't destruction the master plan when you smashed the mirror with that key chain?"

I lay the mirror on the table, huddle over it, try to fit the missing pieces back in, make accidental eye contact with myself, and sit up straight, stop messing with the mirror. "None of your business, Kyle. Stop spying on me."

"You're only at Pilgrim's at all because I let you stay, remember? Show some gratitude."

I take one of the mirror fragments, run the sharp edge experimentally along my palm, but it doesn't feel right, so I put the shard back down. "You're in a good

mood today. Why don't you go run off and play with
your bad company?"

"Don't worry, I'm on my way. Thought I'd warn you
first."

"Warn me of what?"

"Someone's here," Kyle says. "Looking for you."

I feel my heart start racing, but I'm detached, like
I'm hiding inside myself, peering out through my eyes
but not really here. "Who? Where?"

Kyle gestures for me to follow, and although I want
to bolt in the opposite direction, I walk after him, several
steps behind, looking carefully around. I want to run. I
want to head for the elephants, I want to dart underneath them, I want to wrap my arms around a massive
leg and disappear from view, but instead I follow Kyle
because I have to know.

"Lauren told me." Lauren, at the ticket counter. "There
was this guy. He asked about you. He had a picture."

A picture. My heart booms in my ears, a drum, a bass,
heavy, ominous. I falter, start to turn.

"There he is." Kyle points, his back still to me.

I stare at the back of Kyle's head for a long time. My
neck feels too stiff to turn my head, and then I move my
gaze to the right, slowly, bit by bit until I see what he's
pointing at.

I recognize the profile as he leans on the railing by

the crocodile pond, staring down at the sleepy crocs. I swivel around and run, but he has turned around too, he has seen me, and chases after me until he's by my side. I know I can't outrun him. I've tried often enough before. I stop.

Kyle is right behind us. "What's going on?" he asks. "Who is this guy?" He pulls his cell phone from his pocket. "I can call security and have him thrown out."

"Kyle, I assume," Brian drawls. "I heard all about you from that lovely girl at the ticket counter. Prince Charming and Knight in Shining Armor. All rolled into one happy package with animal poop in his hair."

Kyle touches a hand to his hair, then pushes both hands into his pockets, scowling. "Leia? How about I call Dylan to throw him out?" He glares at Brian, who glares back. "Dylan is used to dealing with obnoxious gorillas."

I hold up my hand. "It's okay. Just give us a minute. He'll leave in a minute." I toss my head, gesture for Brian to follow me. I stride to the crocodiles with him following close behind. Kyle falls back but waits, looking at us.

"'Leia,'" Brian says, smirking. "You always liked Mom's silly old movies."

I wrap my arms around myself and stare at the crocs. They're barely moving at all. "What are you doing here?"

"What's with Leia, princess? Is the name Mom picked for you not good enough anymore?"

"Shut up. How did you find me?"

Brian shrugs, holds up a sheet of paper, a printout of the zoo's website. "Spy work. This place was one of the most frequently viewed websites on your computer. And of all the million zoos you've been viewing, this was the closest zoo around. I showed your picture to a girl at the ticket counter, and she said, 'Oh yes, Kyle's girlfriend! She's always around!' Who is that guy Kyle? I can't believe you actually have a boyfriend."

"The girl is called Lauren. What did you tell her?"

"Why, worried about something?"

I yank the page out of his hands, scrunch it together in a ball, toss it in a trash can. "Keep your hands off my computer."

"Aren't you curious about what happened after you disappeared?"

"Not really."

"At first they thought you'd been kidnapped or murdered. Because Aunt Phoebe swore you weren't the type to run away, that you never even liked to leave the house much. But then they found a surveillance tape from a bus station and decided you were a runaway. Aunt Phoebe's pretty freaked out."

"Yeah, I bet she misses me nonstop."

"Why did you run away?"

"None of your business."

Brian's fists bulge the pockets of his jacket. "Was it because of me?"

"No."

"Then what? What made the little mouse leave her little hidey hole?"

"None of your business."

He stares over the fence, at the crocodiles basking in the sun. "I talked to Roz."

"Rosalyn actually spoke to you? It must be snowing in hell."

I bite my teeth together and wait for the blow. Baiting Brian about Rosalyn has never failed to ignite his fury. It doesn't now. His eyes flare up; his face tightens. But he doesn't move. "Roz told me what happened at the Dungeon."

"Nothing happened."

"Who was he?"

"I have no idea what you're talking about."

Brian shuffles. Turns, leans against the railing, stares through the netting at the crocodiles. "Roz told me everything. She told the police, too. Someone came to the café."

I glare at him. Glare at the crocodiles. "It's a café. It has customers."

"She said he was an older man, not a kid from school or anything. He spoke to you. He said something, showed you something." He looks sideways at me. "Roz says he scared you."

"Rosalyn hates you," I say loudly. "She wouldn't tell you anything. She wouldn't give you the time of day. She dumped you, remember?"

Brian's hand slams through the air in my direction. I brace myself, but the punch never reaches me. He spits at me instead. It lands in front of my shoes. Usually he spits in my face. He'd walk right up to me and spit in my face, and he would make me so mad I'd claw at his face or kick him in the shin or yell words designed to slice into him like a dagger, and then I'd run upstairs to my room and lock the door, and he'd come after me and the dust wouldn't settle for hours.

"I hate you," I growl, staring at his spit, sitting on top of the concrete, then wish I could take the words back, because I need him not to turn me in, not to tell anyone anything. "Just leave me alone," I add. "Just go away and leave me alone, and I'll leave you alone."

Brian's eyes are narrowed when he looks at me. "The guy at the café."

"Drop it, Brian!"

"He was one of them, wasn't he?"

I feel like I'm standing on stilts. I no longer sense the ground I'm standing on, and I have no control over my balance. I tilt sideways, land heavily against the fence, grab it. Stare into a crocodile's eye, ten feet away. It isn't blinking. Isn't moving. Just basking, lurking, waiting.

"Wasn't he?" Brian repeats.

"Go away."

"He showed you something," Brian says. "Something from his wallet."

"Shut up."

"It was a picture, wasn't it?"

"Go away."

"He recognized you from a picture, didn't he?"

"Go away!"

"Yeah," Brian says after a while. "He was one of them. And I'm leaving." He pushes himself away from the railing. "Are you ever coming back home?"

My mouth is dry, but I force out words. "I don't know."

"I bet you'll be back when school starts." Brian rolls his eyes. "You must be there, to earn your precious As."

"Shut up. Just because you're too stupid to learn doesn't mean I shouldn't."

I wait for the punch, but it doesn't come. Too many witnesses, perhaps.

"Do you remember—," Brian starts.

"No!"

Brian shrugs. His face blurs. And I feel the wall of air between us, compressed air teeming with poison. With that between us, we can never be closer than this.

He looks at my hands, curled up in fists at my sides. "Do you still do it?"

I lift my hands, open my palms, and hold them out to him. The scars are still there, but no wounds are open. It's healing. "Not recently."

He nods. His right hand grabs his forearm on the opposite side, his fingers trailing over the leather. "Cool."

"I didn't bring my stuff with me," I say. "My box. My needles and the disinfectant and everything . . ." I trail off.

"Needles? Disinfectant? What are you talking about?"

"I don't actually cut, like you do. I just scratch with needles. And needles get dirty. Covered with bacteria. I need to keep the wounds clean . . ." I clamp my mouth shut.

Brian looks away. A muscle in his jaw moves. "I can bring it, I guess," he says. "That box. If you need it. If you tell me where it is, I can go home and get it."

"No." I shake my head. "It's okay. I don't need it anymore. Just . . . don't tell anyone I'm here. Nobody. Not Aunt Phoebe . . . not . . . anyone." My voice is trembling. My legs are shaking at the thought of leaving the zoo. I want to ask him to please, please, please not tell anyone where I am, but begging never makes things any better.

"Right." He reaches into his back pocket. "I've got some money."

A wad of bills is in his hand. I feel the emptiness of the wallet in my back pocket, stare hungrily at the money, imagining all the chocolate Tina and I could buy. "Where did you get money? Do you have a job?"

Brian smirks. "You don't want to know." He shakes the money at me. "Take it. You need money, don't you?"

I stare at the money, but I can't take it. The wall of air is in the way.

Brian's hand opens. The wad of money falls to the ground, nestles against a red-and-white candy wrapper. "Take it or leave it lying on the ground," Brian says. "Makes no difference to me." And he is gone.

CHAPTER EIGHT

Kyle finds me at the seal's pond, hanging on the railing and staring down into their deep-blue pool. The seals are splashing, back and forth, energetic this time of day. In a while they'll crawl up on a stone and bask in the sun, growing warm and heavy and sleepy. They crane their heads and look at me every time they swim past, but I'm not carrying any fish for them this time.

"There's a legend, you know," Kyle says. "That seals carry the souls of drowned fishermen. See how human their eyes look?"

I stare at the creatures playing in front of us. Their eyes are big and brown, warm and trusting. They remind me of Leda. Wide and open. Innocent. Too innocent. It makes me want to grab them, run off, hide them away somewhere before the universe grabs a stick and clubs them on the head, because that's what it always, always does.

"Who was that guy? A boyfriend?"

"No."

"So, who?"

"My brother."

"Oh. Luke?"

"Luke?"

"You know . . . Leia and Luke."

"Yeah . . . well . . . yeah."

"You guys don't look much alike."

"We're twins. Just like Princess Leia and Luke."

"Well, that explains it." He grins, and he's not Brian and there is no wall of poisoned air. For a second the world shimmers into normal and I want to grin too.

"Is he the one you're running away from? Your brother?"

I push myself farther over the railing, stretch toward the water. There's no way I'll ever reach the water unless I actually fall in, but still I stretch, farther and farther. "No."

"Who are you running away from?"

"I don't know."

"A bad guy?"

"Bad," I whisper to the seal straining up out of the water toward me. The zoo seems smaller now, a tiny oasis in shark-infested waters. I can't run away. I can't get away.

I stand upright again, feeling dizzy, clench my hands around the cool metal railing. "What's the most deadly animal in the zoo?" I ask.

Kyle shrugs. "I don't know."

"Guess."

"There are plenty of dangerous animals. The tigers, of course . . . the bears, even. The rhino, the elephants if enraged. But then the tiny ones too. Piranhas, the poisonous snakes or spiders. And of course, chimps, like Tina—they can be dangerous if they want to be. If they're scared or angry."

"What would be the most painful death?"

"You ask weird questions, Leia."

I shake my head hard. My hair falls over my face, warm from the sun, smelling of flowers, the shampoo from the staff showers. I rub my hair across my eyes. "Okay, what's the most pain-free death, then? If you had to be killed by something in the zoo, what would you choose?"

Kyle hooks his arm over the railing, thinking, an interested look on his face. "Well . . . not the snakes or spiders—the poison can be very painful. So is getting ripped apart by a tiger or a bear, I suppose. Unless they go straight for the throat . . . I suppose that would be quick. Most of the time, anyway. I mean, they could decide to snack on your limbs first, and then dig into your liver. Which would be less pain-free, I suppose."

"What about constrictor snakes? You'd pass out, right? From a lack of oxygen? So you'd just fall asleep."

"Get choked to death, get your ribs broken, and then get eaten in one bite and your murderer will probably choke on you. Charming. Help me out here: Which are we planning, a suicide or a murder?"

"If you wanted to kill someone by throwing them in an animal cage, which cage would you choose?"

"This conversation is freaking me out."

"I'm just wondering."

Kyle sighs. "Well, the tigers or the bears, I guess."

"Why?"

"They've got the biggest teeth, less chance of failure. And they're expected to kill. Some of the other animals— if they harmed a person, they might be put down because they're too much of a risk."

I kneel and retie my shoelace, carefully wrap one lace around the other, and finish with a double bow. "Come on," I say, "let's go visit the tigers."

For once I lead and Kyle's the one trailing behind. The tigers lie in shade under the trees, dozing, looking more like cuddly pets than wild killing machines.

"If I go inside, would they eat me?"

"Not sure they'd eat you. They're spoiled, used to their meat landing on the ground in front of them. But they might attack you. They're not used to people inside their habitat. Nobody goes there except Dylan. They might kill you. Or at least do serious injury."

"Why? They get plenty of food. Why would they kill me?"

He shrugs. "It's their nature. They're predators. If something's alive and kicking, they must hunt."

I hook my fingers into the netting, reach through a broken link in the fence, but the second fence is out of reach by several inches. I imagine a tiger strolling up to the net, sitting back and reaching through with a giant paw, extending a claw to meet my stretched-out finger. Our eyes would meet, and we'd stare into each other's souls and realize we didn't want to kill each other. Not today.

"Is the white tiger a separate species, or an albino or something?"

"Neither. It's due to a recessive gene. For a tiger to be white, a cub needs to get that gene from both parents. So it's very rare."

"In danger of extinction?"

"I think so."

"Maybe we need to feed them more humans. We're not in any danger of extinction."

He chuckles. But I'm not making a joke. Some people deserve to be tiger food.

I let go of the netting and turn around. "What if you wanted to get rid of a body?"

Kyle groans. "Are you obsessed with this?"

"Theoretically. Let's say you kill a bad guy, and you need to get rid of the body. Which animal would make the body disappear the best?"

He frowns. "I don't think our PR person ever gets such questions."

"Well, what do you think?"

"The tigers or the bears might eat a dead body if it were fresh. You know, like it's just another pack of meat thrown their way. Not sure they'd feast if the corpse was wearing clothes, though. Their meat tends to be undressed. I bet cotton and denim sticks in your teeth."

He is getting a little too much into the spirit of things. I grimace. "What else?"

"The sharks," Kyle continues. "They'd tear the body apart pretty quick. There would be bone fragments all over their tank, though. And blood. I don't know how quickly blood washes out of their water."

"Okay. Anything else?"

Kyle snaps his fingers. "I know! The piranhas! They would strip the body of flesh, but they'd leave the skeleton. People would assume the skeleton was there for show, so you might get away with it. That would be pretty cool, actually. Hiding the body in plain sight, where hundreds of people look at its skeleton every day."

"The piranhas," I say slowly. "I love it." I stare in the direction of the aquarium and can see it play out on the movie screen in my head. The skeleton forever on display. The empty orbs of the skull staring in desperation at the people passing by, jaws open in a never-ending cry for help, crabs scuttling over outstretched finger bones waiting for a rescue that never comes.

"Forever," I whisper. "Perfect."

Kyle coughs. "What are you talking about? Who do you plan to kill?"

The crazy fantasy is squashed, like a soap bubble under Tina's heavy hand. "No one," I say, my shoulders slumping. "No one at all."

CHAPTER NINE

Another week passes, and I work hard, hide well, play with Tina, play with Leda, gobble up the books Kyle brings me, fill my mind with biology and zoology and nature. I forget about Brian, forget about the piranhas, forget about *I know you*, and when life is nothing but summer and zoo, I'm happy.

"What do you want to be when you grow up?" Kyle asks one day as we leave the elephant habitat and head for the restaurant area to sweep the pavement. "What do you want to do with your life?"

My stomach clenches, and my steps falter as the future opens in front of me, a huge black void gaping open. "I don't know."

"You must have some kind of idea."

I shrug. I'm not sure I will ever be a grown-up. "I don't know. What about you?"

"I'm not sure yet."

"Something to do with animals, I bet?"

"Maybe. Maybe a vet. Maybe a journalist or an activist. I want to tell people about animals, and how careful we need to be or we'll wipe them off the face of the planet. We're like locusts, you see. In old stories they talk about plagues of locusts, leaving nothing but desert in their wake. That's just like us. We leave everything in ruins. The planet is a mess, and it's our fault."

I make a face. "Yes, the planet is a mess. But is it our fault? We're just another species trying to survive. If evolution had been different, if jaguars or llamas could build skyscrapers or send missions to Mars, they would, and they wouldn't worry too much about some freaky hairless apes living in a cave trying to figure out what opposable thumbs are good for."

"But we're ruining this world for ourselves, too! And don't you think we owe the animals something? It's their planet too, and we're destroying their habitats, making it impossible for them to live . . ."

"They destroy each other too. They attack each other, eat each other. They're responsible for other species' extinction. Man isn't the first species to make life difficult for another. We're not the only predators on planet Earth!"

Kyle stares at me like I've sprouted a rhinoceros tusk. "They're just doing it to survive! We know better. We have a conscience, an imagination, intelligence. We know right from wrong. We know what pollution means. We know there are alternative fuel sources. We know we can do things differently."

"We're no different from the animals."

"I thought you liked the animals!"

I charge on, unstoppable now, even though I'm not even sure I agree with myself. "We're greedy. Just like them. Everybody looks out for number one. Every species. Every individual. That's the way things are. You can put all the pretty words on paper that you want, but they won't change anything. Nothing you can do will ever change anything. This is the way the world works. It's the way life works."

"That's not true," Kyle says. "Some people do make a difference. In some ways the world does get better. It can get better . . ."

I shake my head. "It may look that way. But you don't know if anyone really made any difference at all. You've heard that time may be the fourth dimension? Well, it wouldn't make sense that we could control a dimension, would it? We can't control the other three. So why would we be able to control time? If history is a river . . . we're nothing more than droplets splashing into the air. We're inconsequential. Sooner or later we'll go extinct, and the Earth will keep turning, the solar system will keep hurtling through space, and we won't matter, not as individuals, not as a race—and nobody will know or care that we ever existed."

"But—"

We're standing at the restaurant area, arguing so loudly that visitors are staring at us. I grab a broom from the supply cupboard and thrust it at Kyle, then grab another one for myself.

"Nobody matters," I say, almost growling at him. "Nothing matters."

I dawdle on my chores, carefully sweeping up every leaf, every speck of dust, every candy wrapper, every crumb, and bit by bit my mind settles, the mud and dirt sinking to the bottom, leaving the surface clear.

I'm whistling as I sweep the tiles in front of the souvenir shop when out of nowhere, someone's standing there, in scuffed leather shoes and torn jeans, my broom smoothing dust over his toes.

"I ran into your boyfriend," Brian says. "He told me you'd be somewhere here."

I look around, don't see Kyle anywhere, but that doesn't mean he's not somewhere watching, spying.

"What are you doing back here?" I say with a sneer. "Miss me so much?"

"I've been on the lookout for that guy," he says. "The one at the café."

I rub my forehead with my knuckle, feel my stomach clench. "Why?"

"No luck," he continues. "He has vanished."

I hold on tight to the broom. "Why are you looking for him?"

"Roz got a good look at him, and she's been keeping an eye out. He hasn't been back." Brian spits on the ground. "Probably won't be back. She says it looked like you scared him as bad as he scared you. She said he ran out like the devil was after him."

Brian sounds impressed, and I feel small and insignificant, because I didn't do anything. I wish I had. I wish I had been terrifying. I wish I had shot fire with my eyes; I wish I had said something to shrivel him up into a tiny miserable piece of dirt to stomp on.

But I didn't do anything. Anything at all.

"No one's been around asking about you either," he says. "Roz talked to all the staff, and they all promised to let her know if anyone asked about you. No one has. He's too chicken to come back. He's not coming after you. You're safe."

I shrug. "Right."

"So you can come back home."

I resume sweeping. "I don't want to."

"Ever?"

I shrug, turn away, hit a piece of spit-out candy with my broom like it's a golf ball. "Not today."

Brian steps in my way, the broom sweeps over his shoes again. I look up at him and find renewed anger in his features. It's aimed at me this time. "What?" I ask. "I'm not coming home—why do you care? What's wrong, you miss beating me up?"

Brian pulls something out of a pocket, holds it up, close to my face, right against my nose.

"Why did you keep this?" Brian asks, his voice loud, accusing. "Why?"

I tilt my head back until I can focus on the object dangling in front of my eyes. It's a long thin strip, once glossy, cut from a photograph. The strip is narrow, so it's not possible to see any details of the picture it's cut from. It's just random colors now, striped like a cat's tail, dulled by the years and the handling. It was in my room. Under my bed, in a box filled with pens and note-books and stickers and paperbacks. At the very bottom of the box, marking the place in my diary. Brian has gone through my room, through my stuff. He has read my diary. A while ago the thought would have filled me with red-hot rage. Now I don't care.

I shrug.

"You're crazy!" Brian has taken a step closer. His fist tightens around the strip of paper. He's pushing against the wall of air between us, and I move back. "Why would you keep something like that? I thought you wanted to forget. Like I do."

My shoulders feel heavy, but I shrug again.

Brian spits on the ground once more. Wipes his mouth with the back of his hands, contempt ripping through his face. "You want to remember."

"It's not a choice," I say. "I don't want to. I don't like to. I have to."

"Why did you keep this?"

"I need it," I say. Quick as a salamander's tongue, my hand snakes into the poisoned barrier between us, grabs the strip of paper, and pulls. It rips out of Brian's hand, he's left holding a stub. My fingers reel up the long streamer, hide it in my palm. It feels damp, dirty, old.

"Why? Why do you need it?"

"So I'll know it really happened. That I didn't make it up in my head."

"You're crazy," Brian repeats. "Crazy."

"I need this so I know I'm not crazy!" I yell at him.

He slashes a gash in the wall of air, grabs my hand, digs his nails into my skin as he pries one finger at a time open, until the wadded-up strip of paper falls to the ground. He pushes me away hard enough that I stumble and almost fall. He picks up the piece of paper. "I'm getting rid of this."

"No, you're not!"

Brian backs off, turns around, runs. I run after him. I jump at him, grab at his arm. He shakes me off and shoves me away, and I fall to the ground, whimpering in pain as my elbow hits concrete. I run at him again, hang myself on to him, clawing, yelling, stretching to reach what's in his hand, but he's taller than me—he holds his arm up and I can't reach; all I can do is claw at his arm, his face.

A group of people has formed around us. I see Kyle approaching, Dylan in tow, towering over him. Brian sees them too. He shoves me off one last time. I land against the fence. He raises his hand again, and the small ball of paper flies through the air.

Over the fence. Into the tiger den. One of the cubs trots at it and gobbles it up.

"There," Brian says as the tiger cub starts chewing, and he backs away as Dylan speeds up. "It's gone. It's over. Forget now. You have to forget."

CHAPTER TEN

I don't remember running along the paths, past the buildings and the habitats and the visitors and the staff. I climb up onto the hill above the primate area, over a low fence, scramble over the rocky ground and between thorny plants. I throw myself onto soft ground with trees all around, and I hear the noises of the zoo around me, but I don't see anything, anyone, and nobody sees me.

"I am not me," I chant, squeezing my eyes shut, tightening my grasp on the grass. I push my forehead into the ground, feel the blades of grass push into my skin, smell the musty earth. Gravity pulls at me until I can almost feel earth filling my mouth as I disappear into the ground. I dig my nails into the earth, push my palms into the grass. "I am not me," I cry, my teeth clenched, toes of my shoes digging into the grass too, hands clawing, but the earth is fighting back and won't let me in.

The police came to our door late that night so long ago now, asking about an adult in the house, asking about a relative, not telling us anything until Aunt Phoebe was there too, and then the words, lots of words, scary words, *terribly sorry, car crash, off a bridge, both dead.* I remember a grief counselor who spoke a lot, and I sat and watched her mouth move and heard nothing except an invisible waterfall, like I'd stuck my head inside one. I remember the day passing, a minute at a time, and I remember all the weird thoughts that marched through my head. I remember going to bed that evening, putting on my green nightgown with the arithmetic pattern— numbers, pluses, and minuses. I remember climbing into the duvet cover as I always did, and I remember falling asleep and waking when light flashed over my face, and for a moment thinking it had been a dream, that it hadn't been real at all and Mom was still with us, sleeping in her bedroom.

But it was only Brian.

"Quiet!" Brian hisses. "Don't wake Aunt Phoebe." He grabs my wrist and pulls, and I sit up, kicking at the duvet until I'm free. "Come on!"

Brian turns off the flashlight as we pass the guest room where Aunt Phoebe sleeps, and we sneak down the stairs. He turns the flashlight back on to go down the basement stairs, and into the darkroom. He locks the door behind us, and leaves the flashlight on the desk. I lean back against the wall and stare up at the circle of light on the ceiling. It trembles, like we're in an invisible earthquake.

Something scrapes against the floor. Brian has pulled a chair to the middle of the room. He jumps up on the chair and changes the bulb. When he flicks the switch, white light floods the room, a violation. I stare at the lines hanging across the room and can almost hear the developing pictures scream.

Brian is gone when I tear my eyes away from the hanging pictures: the mountain scenes, the flowers and the trees, birds sitting on treetops, squirrels staring into the camera. He has disappeared behind the dark tent separating the developing area from the computer set-up. I hear the hum of the two computers starting up, one after the other, but I don't move. Brian reappears, his hand circles my wrist again. He yanks at the tent, hard, harder, until the sheet tears from the narrow line it was hanging on. He drags me to one of the computers, pushes me down in the chair, his hands cold on my shoulders through my nightgown.

"Delete everything," Brian says as he bends over the other computer, moving from foot to foot and breathing fast as he waits for a program to start. "Everything! Hurry!"

I stare at the screen. The background image is the prize-winning photograph of a horse accepting a lump of sugar from a child. Folders and programs are lined up around the animal and the child.

"Everything," Brian says. "Every folder. Every file. Don't look. Just delete."

My hand moves the mouse, hovering over one folder after another.

"Listen to me!" Brian's voice is hoarse. His hand is icy on my face, turning me to face him, holding tight around my chin. His eyes are red and swollen. I guess mine are too. "Don't you understand? We have to get rid of everything. We have to."

Thoughts are like lava, hot and fiery and unstoppable, pushing out from my core, hissing when hot and cold meet, but sluggish, so very slow. I blink. Brian grabs my shoulders, shakes me. "We must get rid of everything," he repeated. "Don't you see?"

"No . . ."

"The police were here today. They may be back. Or the woman with the briefcase. The social worker. If they see this . . . if anyone sees this . . . everybody will know. It will be in their files, in the police files. People will find out. The newspapers will find out. The kids at school will find out. Everybody will know what happened to us." His fingers dig painfully into my shoulder, and I whimper. "Do you understand? Do you want them to know? Do you? Do you want people to see these pictures?"

I look up at the photographs hanging on the line, swaying from the turbulence caused by our moving bodies. They're lovely. They're art. Prize-winning art. Sunsets, sunrises, mountains, people. Smiles and ice cream and puppies playing in the grass. They're lies. Nothing but pretty lies.

"No," I say dreamily, my gaze fixed on the beautiful pictures. "I don't."

Brian's hand tightens on my shoulder. I whimper from pain, and he pushes me, shoves me toward the computer. "Do it. Delete everything. Everything."

I kneel on the wobbly office chair and get to work. I delete all picture files and documents and e-mail from the computer, then from the flash drives jumbled in a drawer, from the backup drive hidden behind the screen, from the camera memory cards, from the online backup system. Brian kneels on the floor, surrounded by piles of DVDs with numbers and letters scrawled on them with a thick black pen. He hits them with a hammer until they're a million glittering pieces, a treasure hoard of stars sparkling on the carpet. He starts to shove them into an empty box that once held photographic paper, and swears when he cuts himself. He looks up, finds me swiveled away from the computer, and frowns.

"Done?"

I nod. Brian pushes me away, checks my work and,

with a few clicks of the mouse, starts to reformat the hard drive. He leaves the computer working and goes through the cabinets again. His face is red, his hair damp at his temples, his breathing swift and erratic. Fever, Mom would say. But she won't. She will never say anything ever again.

Grief bends me, and I vomit on the floor. Brian curses. "Mom," I whimper.

"Shut up," Brian snarls. "We'll clean up later." He pulls the small shredder from under the desk, pushes it over to the filing cabinet, plugs it in, and yanks the drawer open. "Everything," he says. "Everything in the shredder. Don't look, just shred. Then everything into the bin when the shredder is full."

The shredder makes a low hum when I turn it on. It hisses like a reptile as it slices the first picture. Then I don't hear anything for a while except the blood pounding my ears, my harsh breathing. Don't see anything but the flashes of light dancing off the colors as the pictures slide into the machine. I am a robot, my arms mechanical extensions. I retrieve sheets from the cabinet, slide them into the shredder, again and again. When the red light blinks, I pull the filled shredder open, pour the multicolored ribbons into the bin, close the shredder, and start again. Again. Again.

The computers finish reformatting the hard drives.

Brian turns them off, unplugs them. He unscrews the
back of both machines, fiddles with some wires, yanks
out the two hard drives, puts one on the floor, and hits
it over and over again with a hammer. He pushes the
claw of the hammer into the circuits and scrapes over
them, then hits it again and again until nothing is left
but a flattened mess of metal and plastic. He sees me
looking and pauses. He holds out the hammer, pushes
the second drive across the floor toward me.

I take the hammer. It is heavier than I expected; my
wrist buckles. I clench both fists around the shaft, raise
the hammer high above my head, and slam it down. The
case bends; something inside breaks. I raise my arms
again and bring them down, harder this time. Again.
Again and again and again and again, harder and harder,
until my arms hurt too much to keep going.

Brian takes the hammer out of my limp hands, tosses
it aside, puts both hard drives into the bag along with the
disc fragments. "There is some more junk in the bottom
drawer," he says. "Shred everything. That's the last."

I pull at the drawer. It slides open without a sound,
revealing brown paper envelopes. Too thick to fit into
the shredder. I tear them open, grab a few sheets at a
time, and feed them to the shredder. It doesn't take long.

"Done?"

I nod.

Brian empties the last fragments from the shredder into the bin, carries it out of the darkroom, up out of the basement. Everything is dark and quiet. We tiptoe into the living room, and Brian kneels by the fireplace, his hands moving in the shadowed niche, until tiny flames lick upward.

"I'll keep watch," he whispers. "You burn everything. Hurry. We have to do this fast."

I hear the stairs creak once, twice as Brian takes up his post upstairs. I sit cross-legged by the fire, feel the warmth on my face, the shadows leaping around me, over me. I look into the bin, thrust my hands deep into the well of multicolored strips of paper. The glossy paper catches the light and is beautiful. My eyes focus for the first time tonight. I grab one thin strip and take a look. There is nothing to see in the narrow band. No image, no truth, no lie. It's too thin. All I can see are blended colors. Nothing else, just colors.

I toss the ribbon of paper into the fireplace and watch the flames grab a hold, wrap around it, curling the edges, consuming it, until nothing remains but ashes. I feed the hungry fire another one, and then another, time passing slowly, gloriously, as the small pile of ashes grows bigger.

"What the hell are you doing?"

Brian is back. He swears when he sees the full bin, pushes me away, takes my place, and starts to shovel the scraps into the fireplace, handful after handful. The flames hiss in protest. "We have to hurry!"

"It's beautiful," I say, again dipping my hand into the ocean of shapes and shadows, grabbing a fistful. "Look! Look at all the colors!"

Brian grabs my wrist, squeezes until I whimper, and my fist opens and releases the shredded fragments. He flings my hand away from the bin. I feel one strip of paper glued to my palm, make a fist, and hide it behind my back. Brian doesn't notice. He is too busy throwing handfuls of paper into the fireplace.

"Go stand watch upstairs," Brian says. But I don't do as he says. I sit back and stare at the fire eating up all the colors, and when Brian leaves, carrying the empty bucket, I still sit there, my hand curled tight around the last strip of glossy paper. My eyes water from the warmth of the fire. The smoke curling up from the pile of ashes is black. I clench my fist tighter around the last fragment of a picture, close my eyes, and fly, slip up the chimney, follow the smoke up into the sky, up, up, up, higher and higher. I wait for the smoke to disperse and disappear, but it never does, and neither do I.

CHAPTER ELEVEN

I push my face deeper into the ground, breathe in earth, and try not to think—then my body can't stand it any longer, can't stand being still, can't stand not thinking, can't stand not running, and I spring to my feet, run again, fast, fast, as fast as I can until my legs tremble and my lungs ache. The sun is still shining, but it feels dark and cold, like a malignant cloud is strapped to my head.

I end up at the back of the elephant habitat, use my key, and sneak in. A bucket of fruit is sitting on the floor, ready for the elephants' next snack. I haul the bucket toward the back, behind the trees, where the animals have a place to hide from zoo visitors if they want to. Calliope is there, and Leda, and I sink to the ground and sit by Calliope's front leg, trembling less and less as I feed them one fruit after another, as much as they want, anything they want. I'm too close to the animals, not careful enough; I'm ignoring all the rules Kyle taught me, but I don't care—I don't mind if they crush me, don't mind at all.

"What happened? What's wrong?" Kyle is kneeling in

the dirt, reaching out to me, and I realize he's been here for a while, talking to me, and I didn't notice. "Leia?" He touches my hand. Just his fingertips, just for a moment, but it's warm and real and wonderful for a second before it's dark and horrible and frightening, and I yank my hand away. His hands are dark, very tanned; mine are lighter because before I came to Pilgrim's, I used to hide them inside my sleeves all the time. I rub my forehead with the back of my hand, and it comes away damp with sweat. I stare at the moisture streaking over the dirt on my shaking hands.

"Did you tag me with a GPS transmitter or something?" I snarl at him.

"You're not that unpredictable," he shoots back. "You disappear and all I have to do is look either here or with Tina."

"You're not my keeper."

"You're in trouble, aren't you?"

I shrug.

"Is it your brother? I saw you fight. And you freak out every time he comes here. Is he the problem? Is he beating you up?"

"He's not the problem."

"Something else, then? Someone else?"

"Yeah."

Kyle's biting his lip, frowning, looking exactly like he

does when he's having trouble getting the baby orangu-
tan to feed, and it almost makes me want to smile. "It's
bad, isn't it? Really bad trouble?"

I shrug.

"Maybe I can help. Maybe Mom can help. If someone's doing something to you . . . whatever it is . . .
maybe we can fix it."

"You can't fix me," I say. Something's heavy inside me.
Lead, lining my insides, a thick layer of lead stretched all
across my skeleton. "I wish you could. I'm not in danger.
Not anymore. I'm just . . . wrong. I'm broken. Everything's
wrong with me. But you can't fix it. Nobody can."

"What happened?"

"Bad people," I say. "Bad things. It was a long time ago."

"Long time ago? What about that guy you're running
away from?"

"He's nothing. He's only an echo." I swallow the salty
water filling my mouth, tilt my head back, and look up
at the sky. It's blue, cloudless, and I know the stars are
there, even though they can't be seen in the light of day.
"Did you know that echoes can travel for eons across the
universe? Almost forever. There are even echoes of the
birth of the universe. You're never free of echoes."

"The bad people . . . did they catch them?"

I shake my head. "It doesn't work that way, Kyle.
They only catch bad guys in the movies. In real life it

doesn't happen that way. In real life the bad guys get away. Most of the time nobody even tries to catch them."

I push myself off the ground, walk to Calliope where she's rubbing against a tree, and maneuver until I'm standing between her front legs, resting my hand on each one, feeling the thick barklike texture of her skin.

Maybe if I hurt enough, and heal enough, and hurt again and heal again, my skin will grow tougher and tighter and thicker until they'll need a sniper with a custom-made bullet to bring me down. Maybe I can become an elephant when I grow up. I wrap my arms around Calliope's left leg, run my tongue over my front teeth, imagine my teeth growing, pushing out of my mouth as giant tusks with deadly points.

"Leia?"

My heart jumps up, hits my brain hard enough to knock me out of the fantasy. "What?"

Kyle looks sad. Helpless. "Do you want to . . . I don't know . . . talk about it . . . or something?"

"No." The movie starts, playing in my head, and won't stop. I keep my eyes open to let in the light, and stare at the elephants, who are bigger, stronger, real, and right there. I try not to blink because movies are clearer in darkness. "I can't."

Kyle looks down. His hands rest on a large stone between us, tanned and dirty. My hands tremble because

I want to reach out and touch him, but he's from a world I'm just visiting and I don't dare. "Okay," he says. "Sorry. Never mind."

I sigh. My breath trembles in disappointment. "Tell me something," I say, rubbing my eyes until colors bleed across my vision. "Tell me something to stop the thoughts."

"What thoughts?"

"Tell me something," I beg, because the pictures are getting brighter, louder. I squirm, itching everywhere, and push myself against Calliope, wanting to claw, scratch, until a rush of pain means everything's gone. "Tell me anything. Tina. Talk about Tina."

"Okay . . . Ah . . . They were talking about Tina at yesterday's meeting. I eavesdropped. The news isn't good."

It works. The pictures fade, vanish, are gone, and the accompanying soundtrack in my head subsides. I let go of Calliope, and everything's forgotten for a while. "What?"

"The sanctuaries are overflowing—no one has promised to take her in yet. She's on waiting lists, and Mom's going to try a few more places, but it sounded like they were close to giving up."

"What do you mean, giving up?"

Kyle looks down at the ground. "You know what they mean. They're talking about putting her down."

"Killing, you mean. You're killing her."

"I'm not doing anything. It's not my decision, Leia— or whatever your name really is."

"You could stop them. You could talk to your mom, convince her. She's a good person. I can't believe she wants to kill Tina."

"Mom is always trying to do what's best for the animals. She never puts anyone down without a good reason. Tina has made progress, but she is still suffering. She can't stay here at Pilgrim's; she would never tolerate living in a zoo. And we can't keep her in quarantine forever."

"So? So what if she's suffering? If you're suffering, have you forfeited your right to live? To heal?" Crazy fantasies rush through my head. Of opening Tina's cage, taking her hand, walking side by side out of the cage and into the world, free, completely free. I know it's crazy. But it's what I want to do. Save Tina. Save Tina at all costs.

"They can't do it!" I scream. Behind me Calliope makes a worried sound.

"They're just talking about euthanasia. They haven't made a decision."

"Euthanasia? You mean, murder!" I yell. "Tell it like it is. Murder!"

"She's suffering. If we can't find a way to help her—"

"Everybody suffers!" I shout, forgetting all about the rule of no loud noises. Beside me Calliope moves restlessly as if to warn me, and I listen to her. "Humans suffer too," I hiss at Kyle in a lower tone. "Everybody hurts! We don't walk around giving overdoses to the sick or the old or the abused or the crazy, do we?"

"Well, maybe we should," Kyle growls back. He turns his back to me, strides to the exit. "I'm not sure needless suffering is a human right I want!"

I feel tears in my eyes; for the first time in forever, my eyes are not dry. "They can't kill Tina. They can't, Kyle. We can't let them do this to her. Please . . ."

Kyle looks back over his shoulder, and his anger is gone. "I'm sorry, Leia. I already tried talking to my mom. I really tried."

"And?"

He shakes his head. "They're giving her another month, but if we don't hear from the sanctuaries, that will probably be the end."

CHAPTER TWELVE

I have spent a lot of time at Tina's habitat, but I have never been on her side of the bars. I turn the handle without hesitation, but the door keeping us apart turns out to be locked, even though there is another locked door leading to the staff area. Double security or perhaps they think Tina might open the door herself. I fish my key chain out of my pocket. Try the small key, and am lucky: The lock opens. I push at the door.

One step and I'm inside.

This is a strange place, an outdoor habitat surrounded by buildings. Being inside means being outside. And when you go outside the habitat, you are actually going inside.

Tina is sitting under her tree, watching me. She doesn't seem upset that the door opened.

"Hello," I whisper. I'm not afraid. I know Tina won't hurt me.

I hope she knows I won't hurt her.

I sit down, my back against the bars I used to pass food and toys through.

Between us, no bars, no walls. Only trees and a metal

bucket and her toys, scattered around, ropes hanging between the trees. Against the opposite wall Tina sits, staring at me. I wonder if she knows I'm on the inside now, if she can distinguish between outside and inside; I wonder if she knows she's locked away. There's so little I know about how animals think. I want to read more books. I want to meet more animals.

We sit together for a long time, looking across, not exactly at each other but in the general direction. Once in a while she tosses things my way, a pebble, a branch, and I toss something back. Every now and then she stands up and shuffles closer, and every time, I also move forward a foot or two. I should have brought my soap bubbles, but the container is still empty in my pocket—I forgot to get more soap.

"What the hell are you doing?"

I recognize Kyle's voice, but I don't turn around. I hear him swear and curse, and I flash back a hand signal, silently telling him to leave me alone.

"Mom saw you in the elephant habitat," he mutters. "She found out about you feeding them by yourself in the morning. I'm grounded until I'm twenty-five. Now get out of there, or I won't be getting my driver's license until I'm thirty."

"Just leave us alone," I whisper, maintaining eye contact with Tina.

"Leia, get out of there now!"

"No. Just go away and leave us alone."

"Mom's going to kill me," he moans. "Get out, Leia. Please. Now."

"Go shovel something."

"You don't know what you're doing," Kyle whispers. "I know you like her, but she's unpredictable. That makes her dangerous. She could hurt you without meaning to. And she's strong. Very, very strong, much stronger than she looks. Now, I'm going to open the door, okay, and you back away slowly, and get out of there. Don't turn your back on her—just back out of there."

I ignore him.

Kyle sighs. "What are you doing in there, anyway?"

"Bonding."

He swears. "Leia. You don't know what you're doing. She's a wild animal, unpredictable because she's been abused, many times stronger than you are. You're not safe in there. Please. You could get hurt."

I don't answer him. Tina's yawning, but I can sense that she's tensing up. Kyle's upsetting her. I hear him open the door, and I shuffle forward on my knees, moving closer to Tina. I hear the door close, and he's behind me, sitting by the wall. "Okay," he says in resignation. "I'm on board. I suppose this has something to do with saving Tina. But exactly what are we doing inside her habitat, where nobody is ever supposed to go?"

"I want to show her that we're safe. That she's safe with us."

"We're not safe. She's not safe. We're her captors. Her fate is whatever we decide. We're keeping her imprisoned, and we shoot her with a tranquilizer dart when we need to move her or treat her. We're afraid of her, and she knows it. And she won't hesitate to attack us if she feels threatened. And she always feels threatened—you know she does."

"No . . . ," I whisper. "We're helping. She must know we're trying to help. She must know we love her—she understands so much."

"Leia, please, come with me out of there. I'll talk to Mom about Tina. I have a plan. I'll start an online petition to save Tina. Once we get her picture and her story out, there will be public pressure to save her. They won't put her down when thousands of concerned citizens know her name and that sad face."

I stare at Tina's face. She doesn't flinch at Kyle's words, but I'm sure she understands.

"And I'll ask Mom to make you a part of the Tina project," Kyle continues. "You know Tina better than anyone—Mom knows that. Maybe she'll listen to you. We can tell her you want to be a vet or something. We'll forge permission from your guardian or something.

Come on. If Mom catches us in here, if she catches you in here . . . it won't help you and it won't help Tina."

Kyle is right. A small ray of sense shines through the thunderclouds in my head. This isn't helping Tina. And I'm ruining my chances to stay on at Pilgrim's Zoo. And if I'm banned from the zoo, I can never help Tina at all.

"Okay," I say, standing up, and I hear Kyle sigh in relief. I back toward the door as Kyle instructed, my gaze on Tina. I'm not watching where I'm going.

I stumble on something, wave my arms frantically trying to regain balance, but fail. I fall, trying to grab at the bars, but they are too far away. My knee hits something hard that skips away. I hear a loud crash.

Tina screeches. I smell her close by. And Kyle screams.

Kyle's hands lock onto my wrists. He drags me toward the door, away from Tina, who has turned into a monster, yelling as she jumps up and down. We're out. The door slams shut after us. Kyle's breathing heavily. There's blood on his hands, my hands, on our clothes.

"What happened?"

"The bucket," Kyle says. "You hit the bucket with your foot, and it rolled over and crashed into the fence. Tina panicked."

"She's hurt. There's blood! We need to get a vet! Call someone!" I clench the bars, stare at Tina, scanning for injury.

"Don't worry," Kyle says dryly. "Tina's safe. It's only my blood."

I twist around and look at him. His hand is bleeding. He pulls his sleeve forward and wraps the cuff around his hand, grimacing in obvious pain.

Tina has moved up into a tree, hugging a branch, still making loud noises, fear and anger indistinguishable. I dry the blood off my hands. I don't even have a scratch.

"The sound scared her. She probably associates loud noises with being beaten. So she defended herself and bit me." He swears. "I need to go find Mom. I'll need a tetanus shot, so I'll have to tell her what happened."

He's not saying "I told you so," but he doesn't need to. My palms throb as I stare at Tina, wondering if I've hurt her. "What will happen to her now? Will they kill her? Will they kill her for biting you?"

"Mom is more likely to kill me," Kyle mutters. "If I don't die from rabies or something first. She's going to scream 'You should know better!' until the day I die." He pulls a face when he looks at me. "I was kidding. Don't faint on me. I'm not going to die from rabies. Mom's not going to kill me. Mom's in her office. She'll fix me up."

"I'll come with you."

Kyle gives me a look and starts walking. "Don't bother."

I can't help myself—I follow Kyle as he strides toward the administrative building, occasional drops of blood dripping on the ground. Eve's sitting at her desk, leaps up when she sees us.

"What happened?"

"A tiger needed a snack," Kyle says. "It's not serious. Looks worse than it is."

"A tiger bit you? You went into the tiger habitat? Are you serious? Why? How did that happen, Kyle? How?"

"Told you," Kyle says in my direction. "She's more furious than concerned about her only child's well-being."

"Kyle, you have been brought up in this zoo. You should know better!"

"Told you she would say that," Kyle says with a smirk.

Eve almost growls at him in frustration. "Let's take a look at that hand."

She pushes him across the hall into a small examining room. Kyle sits on the bench as his mom cleans the wound and applies a bandage.

"This doesn't look like a tiger bite," Eve says. "But if a tiger really did this, you had a very lucky escape."

Kyle shrugs.

Eve looks at him, looks at me. I stand in the door, not sure what to do. This was my fault. I should be the one in trouble, not Kyle. Yet I'm not brave enough to confess this was my fault. And I can't tell her Tina did this. I can't risk Tina's life.

"You'll need shots," Eve says to Kyle.

"Yeah. I know."

Eve leans back when she has finished bandaging the wound, crosses her arms, and frowns at Kyle. "Explain yourself."

"What's the point?" Kyle says. "I made a mistake. I know that. I've made mistakes before. I know the drill. I regret it; it won't happen again."

I've taken a few steps back, hoping to disappear into the dark corner.

Eve takes a deep breath. "Tell me what you were thinking when you went in there."

Kyle shrugs. "I thought I would be fine," he mutters.

"Do you want me to ban you from Pilgrim's? Take away your keys? Is that what you want?"

"I made a mistake, okay? I told you—it won't happen again."

Eve looks at me, notices the blood on my sleeves. "Are you hurt too?"

"No." I shake my head. "It's Kyle's blood. It's my fault, not his. I wanted to . . . I just wanted to . . ."

"Leia, did you go into the tiger cage?"

"No," I say honestly. "But . . ."

"You have been in some of the other habitats. Without permission."

"It's not Kyle's fault . . ."

If I thought this would help, I'm mistaken. Eve turns back to Kyle. "You put her life at risk. I'm so disappointed in you."

"But—," I start, but Kyle's gaze shoots a command at me, and I shut my mouth before I say something else that won't help.

"I'm sorry, Mom. It won't happen again."

"You're off zoo duty this week at least. I'll find other chores for you. I'm taking away your keys for now. If you ever get them back, it will be probational. And if I ever see Leia or another friend of yours inside an animal habitat without permission, you will never get your keys back. Understood?"

Kyle nods, but Eve has already stormed out the door. He grimaces when the door slams shut behind her. "Ouch. Don't worry. Her bark is worse than her bite."

"I'm banned from the habitats," I say, reality rising like a wall in front of my face. "From Tina. From Leda. From everything. I can't meet any of them ever again."

Kyle cradles his bandaged hand in the pit of his arm and grins. "Don't worry. We still have your keys."

CHAPTER THIRTEEN

The butterfly house is hot and humid. I find a place to sit within the small jungle, where I can't be seen from the roped-off path the zoo visitors follow. Sweat forms on my forehead, my neck, trickles down my back. My clothes get damp, but I just sit there. It's silent in here, apart from the low drone of the machines responsible for the heat and the humidity. I draw in a damp breath. Water is trickling everywhere; underneath I hear a hum of motors. There's no stink, like most places in the zoo—only the sweet smell of rotting fruit and foreign flowers.

Some butterflies don't eat at all. They are born, they procreate, and they die of starvation. It's hard to see the point, but I guess eating doesn't add much point. Neither does talking or praying or watching TV.

Kyle won't find me in here. He won't even search inside buildings like this one, because he thinks I'm afraid of ceilings and walls. I can sit here forever without him finding me.

One by one, butterflies land on me, until a dozen are

sitting on me, on my legs, my shoulders, my hair. They sit still for ages, antennas barely quivering. I don't know why they decided to sit on me, what they're thinking. It's not like I have any pollen for them. Maybe they're sleeping. They probably don't have brains big enough to be thinking.

The heat makes me thirsty, and in the end I give in, find a vending machine, and spend some of my last coins on a soda. I head toward the elephants because that's where I feel safest, but I don't make it all the way, because a familiar figure sits on a bench outside the aquarium.

"Go away, Brian," I say. I throw the almost-empty soda can at him. Dark fluid splutters at his feet. "Go away. Leave me alone."

Brian looks behind me. "Do you live in that guy's pocket or something?"

I twist around. Kyle is here, behind me, staring at my brother. He must have been following me. Watching out for me. I want to roll my eyes, but they're watering.

"I guess you must be Luke," Kyle says.

"Luke?" Brian looks at me, back at Kyle, then grins. "Leia's brother. Right. I'm Luke."

"Did you run away too?" Kyle asks.

"How much have you told your boyfriend here?" Brian asks.

I feel my face turn bright red. I can't look at Kyle. "Shut up," I hiss at my brother.

"She's never had a boyfriend before," Brian explains to Kyle. "Too shy. You should see her at school. She nearly squeezes into the walls when she walks down the hallway. And if someone tries to talk to her, her face turns white and then red, and she looks like they're about to drag her into a gas chamber."

I turn my back and stride away, but Brian doesn't fall into step behind me. When I look back, the two of them are sitting together on that bench, Brian gesturing as he talks. Gesturing toward me, like he's talking about me.

I hurry back, because the one thing worse than having Brian talk to Kyle about me is him doing that when I'm not there to do damage control. I grab my brother's arm and pull him away. When he looks down at my hand circling his wrist, I quickly let go of the warm leather.

"Don't," I say. "Go away. Just go away. Leave him alone. Leave me alone."

"You like him," Brian says. "You like him," he says in a singsong voice, and I want so badly to kick him.

"What are you doing back here?"

"Visiting my crazy sister at the animal asylum."

"Go away."

"I'm finished with you. Do you even know what day it is today?"

I have no idea. I have lost track of time. I only know Mondays because the zoo opens later. I think it's still July, but I'm not sure.

"Four years today," Brian tells me. "It's August first. Four years."

Mom. I whimper as the word scrapes across my mind. *Mom.*

"No candle in the window for her this year, princess? No red rose on her grave, Mommy's girl?"

"Shut up."

"You said you want to remember, sis. You want to remember so you know that you're not crazy. Well, remember Mom, too. Remember what she did."

"She didn't do anything."

"Exactly."

"She couldn't do anything. She didn't know. She couldn't . . ."

"It wasn't quite like that, Princess Leia," Brian says with a sneer. "You want to remember. Remember that, too."

I remember.

It is just me and Mom and Brian at home, and we've been fighting, and Mom tries to intervene, and then Brian and Mom are yelling, Brian yelling nasty things from the top of the stairs while Mom cries in the kitchen. He yells curses, insults, bleeding words, and once in a while she yells back, telling him to shut up, threatening him, at last yelling at him at the top of her lungs, telling him to just wait until he gets home.

And then Brian says it. He tells her what happens while she's working shifts downtown. He tells her what's in the file cabinet in the basement. He uses words I didn't know could be spoken—he shouts it out, it echoes down the stairs and throughout the house, and then a throbbing silence fills my ears.

My blood turns to molasses in my veins as I wait for Mom's answer. I hear her walk to the stairs, up a step or two. I hear her hiccup a laugh, a low fake laugh, like when she laughs at a lame joke, a joke that's not really funny, or maybe one she doesn't understand. I hear her call up. "What did you say?"

I hold my breath. I feel like my world is a tiny metal capsule, about to burst, projecting deadly fragments in all directions.

Brian is silent. He doesn't repeat his accusation, doesn't retract his words either. The stairs don't creak, so Mom hasn't moved up or down. She is still standing there, halfway up, halfway down, and not saying anything either.

My lungs are screaming for oxygen by the time I hear the stairs creak again. She is heading down, not up.

Nothing more happens.

Breath leaves my body in a silent explosion. My world is still here, the metal capsule intact, forgotten for now but still deadly.

"I told her what was going on, remember?" Brian growls. "I told her, straight out, and she didn't believe me. She even laughed it off, like a joke."

"She didn't hear you," I say, hiccupping around the words burning up my throat because I want so badly to believe what I'm saying. "She didn't hear what you said. She asked you what you'd said. You didn't repeat it. It's your fault. Your fault! If you'd repeated it . . ."

"She heard me the first time. She didn't want me to repeat it. She didn't want to hear it. She may not have been on his side, but she sure wasn't on our side either. She never even tried."

"We don't know. Maybe she did . . . We don't know what happened the day they died. We don't know. . . ."

"On the day she died? What has that got to do with it?"

I feel my chin tremble, like I'm five years old.

Brian looks at me wryly, pity and anger and disgust taking turns on his face. "So that's what Mommy's girl has been hoping all this time."

I turn away from him.

"You're hoping the accident was no accident," Brian continues. "You're hoping she drove off that bridge on purpose. You're hoping she made an ultimate sacrifice, for us."

It's my secret dream, one I dare not think about too much, and I blink in the glare of Brian's intrusion, cower when he smears dirt all over my fantasy.

"Seriously?" Brian sneers. "That's actually what you've been hoping. How stupid can you be?"

"It could have," I hiccup weakly. "It could have happened that way. Nobody knows what happened. Nobody knows what she—"

"She wasn't even driving, Princess Leia. I've read the accident report. It's in the drawer with our birth certificates and all the other documents. Haven't you read it yourself?"

I shake my head hard, deny everything.

"The insurance company made sure there was a thorough investigation before they coughed up the life insurance money. You know Mom hardly ever drove when she was with him. And she wasn't driving that day."

My mind swerves, looking for options, exits, rays of hope. "Maybe she grabbed the wheel. She could have grabbed the wheel and—"

"Yeah. Right. She *could have*. She *could have* done pretty much anything at any time, right?"

I hold my hands over my ears. I don't want to hear Brian's sarcasm.

"Mom didn't save us," he says flatly, pulling both my hands away from my ears, holding them tight so I have no choice but to listen. "Face it, Princess Leia. Nobody saved us. Nobody even tried to save us. Mom never did anything. We just got lucky. We got lucky they died."

CHAPTER FOURTEEN

I hear Kyle yell my name as I run past him, yell my stupid pretend name, but I can't stop, I won't stop—I'm running and I don't know where. In here I can only go in circles, and this time not even the elephants can protect me.

I stop when the stitch in my side starts pinching at my insides, sit down at an abandoned picnic table. I curl my fingers into my palm, rub the scarred flesh with my fingertips, need, need, need to cut, to scratch, need it so bad for the first time in ages.

I have nothing anymore. I don't have my elephants, I don't have Tina, and I don't have my box. I don't have my needles and the rubbing alcohol and the cotton balls. Heat fills my eyes, salty water fills my mouth, drops leak from my chin and darken the sun-bleached wood of the table.

I could have stopped by at home before getting on the bus that day. I could have gone home first and gotten my box. How could I leave something so important behind? Brian even offered to bring it to me. And I said no. I thought I didn't need it anymore.

Stupid. Stupid, stupid.

I look at my hands, stare into them. Even if I find a needle or a knife, it's not enough. I'm not clean enough. There's dirt under my fingernails, and my hands are filthy all the time. Bacteria everywhere. Washing isn't enough. I need my box. I need the disinfectant and the sterile needles.

I can't go back to get it.

My hands feel heavy and thick, filled with blood that wants out. I push them in my pocket and raise my face to the sun. My tears evaporate in a few seconds, leaving a tiny amount of salt lacing my cheeks.

I wonder if Tina would cut if she were better at using tools. I think about her leathery palms and shiver, don't want to imagine them split open, don't want to imagine the drops of chimp blood oozing out of the fresh wound. Red blood, like mine.

I want my box. I need my box.

There's a security guard outside the office building, but he knows me, knows my uniform T-shirt, saw me enter with Kyle before. I try to look normal and it works; he smiles and nods when I walk up the stairs as if I belong there. I hear voices from inside one office, and duck into the small room where I watched Eve clean Kyle's wounds. It's got a small examining table, drawers, cabinets. I yank

a few drawers open until I see what I need: sterile pack-
ages of hypodermics, bottles of disinfectant. I usually
use sewing needles. But these will do too. I grab two
hypodermics and a bottle of disinfectant, turn around,
and am running for the door when it opens.

"Leia?" Eve stares at me, surprise first, then disappointment, then horror when her gaze slides down to
the loot I'm hugging to my chest.

"Hypodermics. You're stealing hypodermics." She
sags, one hand still on the doorknob, blocking my way
out. "Oh no, Leia, you're . . ."

I shake my head. "I'm not stealing them for . . . I'm
not a junkie."

"Kyle?" She's suddenly pale. "Is Kyle using? I wasn't
sure, but I hoped he hadn't gone that far. . . . Is he?"

"No!" I shake my head. I've gotten Kyle in too much
trouble already. "He's not. Honest. And Ti—the tiger
thing, it wasn't his fault. It's all my fault. Just me."

Eve glances to her side at a small door, and her hand
goes to her pocket, feels for keys, phone. "Hypodermics,
disinfectant . . . what do you need those for if it's not
drugs?"

"I can't tell you. But I'm not doing drugs. I promise."

"I see." She talks to me, takes the stuff out of my
arms, and puts everything down on the table. She raises
her hands to me but backs off when I flinch. "If you're

telling me the truth, I'm sure you don't mind me looking at your arms."

"What?"

Her gaze is steady on me, but she radiates with fear
for Kyle. "If you're not planning on using those needles
to shoot up, you won't mind me taking a look at your
arms for needle marks."

I open my mouth to protest, but then I think of Kyle.
I grit my teeth and hold my arms out, my hand curled. I
hope she won't look at my palms.

Eve pushes my sleeves up, takes my wrist. I close my
eyes, tremble at the touch. Her hand is warm, human,
comforting, yet so frightening. She turns my arm and
peers at it. "Okay. No needle marks." She peers into my
eyes; her fingers push against the pulse in my wrist. "No
overt signs. What do you need this stuff for, then?"

"I just wanted them," I mumble. "I need them. I
need . . ."

"Kleptomania? You're stealing because you like to
steal?"

"No! I just need a couple of needles. That's all."

"But you won't tell me why." Eve lets go of me and
steps back. She rubs the bridge of her nose. "Look . . .
there's something going on here. With you. I'm trying
to trust my son, but . . . I can't ignore this any longer. I
need to talk to your parents."

"My parents are dead."

"Your guardian, then. Or else the police. Child welfare authorities. As a responsible adult I have to think of
your well-being, and you're obviously in trouble, Leia,
and I want to help. The correct way to help is to bring in
the authorities to help you."

"Don't," I whisper. "Please don't . . ."

"You've been living here at the zoo, haven't you?"

I stare at the tiles.

Eve sighs. "I feel guilty for keeping my eyes closed
this long. It's obvious. You're always around. You haven't
left the zoo in weeks. Have you?"

I shrug. Don't look up. Feel her gaze on me for a
long time. "What is it?" she asks gently at last. "What is
wrong? I promise, I will try to help. What's the trouble?
Something at home?"

"I can't go back. I can't. Please." My voice is cracking.
"Please, don't make me . . ."

"Are you unsafe at home? Is someone hurting you?"

"I can't go home."

"Leia, if you can't go home, the authorities can find
you some kind of a foster home, people to look after
you. Maybe a boarding school or something . . . I'll talk
to them, if you like. We'll work something out. It'll be
for the best, I promise."

"Just until the end of summer," I say, and I hear my

voice quiver with desperation. "Please. Let me stay until the end of summer, and then I'll go."

"Go where?"

"Home," I say, staring down at the striped linoleum. "I'll go home. When summer is over. I don't need foster care or a boarding school. I can go home. Just not yet."

Eve is silent for a few minutes. "Will you be safe?" she asks. "At the end of summer, will you be safe going home?"

I nod. "I can't go now. I need to stay a while longer. Before school starts, I'll go. I promise, I'll go home then."

"I have to do something," she says. "I'm liable. Legally and ethically. If something happens to you . . . As a responsible adult I can't . . ."

I feel tears slide down my cheeks as I look at her. She has brown eyes just like Kyle does. She breaks off after a long pause, sighs, turns her back on me, braces her hands on the counter, and stares out the window. I wait for a long moment before I realize she's giving me an opportunity. Whether it is on purpose or not.

I look at the needles and disinfectant on the table between us.

I clench my hands and feel the tainted blood throbbing in my overfilled palms, screaming to get out.

I grab the stuff and run.

Eve lets me go. Nobody chases after me. I go to my favorite hiding place, crawl beneath the lowest branches to get to a tiny clearing deep within a cluster of trees. Calmness wraps around me like a warm blanket as I pour disinfectant into a paper cup from one of the staff vending machines, as I tear the wrapper off one needle and drop it in. Unlike my sewing needles at home, these needles are already sterile in their wrappings, but the ritual is comforting, safe, almost like standing beside Calliope with my arms wrapped around her leg.

While the needle soaks, I open my palm and stare at the lines. My lifeline, starting between my thumb and my forefinger, extending toward my wrist. The other lines, slashing across my palm. They're probably called something, but I don't know what. Then there are the new lines, lines I made myself, white and silver scars, white spots, where I scratched and poked with needles in my room back home. Nothing's open anymore, nothing's red and swollen, but that will change now.

I fish the sterile needle out of the cup, close my eyes, and rake the sharp point over my palm, but I don't feel the usual shiver of anticipation when the needle scratches my skin. I push harder, but the soft sting of pain doesn't come.

I drop the needle back into the cup, flex my hands, open them, and look beyond the lines and the scars.

My palms have changed. The skin is thick and leathery, almost like Tina's. I have calluses from the shovel and the ropes and the buckets and brooms, from all the work I've been doing here.

I rub my hands together, listen to the sandpaper sound the rough skin makes. Again I grab the needle, push the point against my palm, but it doesn't break the skin. I push harder, and the needle slides into the thick skin, but I don't feel it. I don't feel anything, and no blood oozes from the tiny hole.

The heaviness drains from my hands. I am filled with wonder instead.

I lean back against the tree and hear birds chirping, invisible in the crown of leaves above my head. I feel the warmth of the air on my skin, smell the earth and the animals, feel life sparkle and ignite inside my chest. I draw my legs up, prop my arms on my knees, and stare into my palms, smiling at my gift from Pilgrim's Zoo.

I have elephant hide.

CHAPTER FIFTEEN

Eve and I have made up. I've returned what I stole, explained what I could, and apologized. The leaves are changing color, and today is Kyle's last day working here. Tomorrow he goes back to school. My school will be starting soon too.

And I promised Eve, promised myself, that before then I will return home.

I lie in the grass in my hiding place and stare up at the darkening sky, imagine the millions of stars I'd see if it weren't for the photopollution from the city. I imagine one star after another blinking out, gone forever, but nobody ever notices because new ones are born in their place.

That's how nature works, one of Eve's books says. Our genes are the travelers. We're just the vessel, all of us, all living creatures. There is no course laid in, no ultimate destination. Just a journey.

My head feels heavy on the ground. A straw tickles the back of my neck. Or maybe an insect, feeling its way across my skin. Maybe I feel the soft sting of a greedy vampire bug, stealing a drop of the red oil lubricating my system, just another vessel in need of fuel, another traveler doing whatever it takes to keep going.

If I look hard enough, I think I can see the occasional star, even with the glare of the city lights.

Every day, down here on the planet, a species goes extinct. A traveler goes down a blind road and perishes. These days we're the ones who construct most of the roadblocks. And the stars, blinking in and out of existence without us noticing, are ancient history, a lost message from a thousand years ago. In the great scheme of things, light doesn't travel all that fast.

It's almost closing time, almost time.

I stand up, brush grass and insects off my clothes, and walk backward down the path of evolution toward the Orange exit. I will not say good-bye to anyone, because I will be back—I will be back all the time.

I pass the elephants, and Kyle is playing with Leda, and I can tell by the way he pretends not to see me that he has been waiting for me to pass. He knows I'm leaving; he knows I will be back. I raise my hand, not in a wave good-bye, only a connection, and he looks up and smiles. We have started our online "SAVE TINA!" campaign. We have thousands of supporters already.

The Orange exit is busy, people flocking out, some with tired children half-asleep on their shoulders. I haven't looked beyond the gates for a long time, but out there is life, a busy pedestrian street. I stare as if it's a new habitat, with a new and interesting species I've been waiting to meet.

The streetlights have come on. The weather is still warm, and the street is crowded with people. Children in shorts and T-shirts, with ice cream stains on their chests. Kids my age, couples, holding hands, grinning at each other. Trees, people sitting on benches in their shadow.

I walk closer.

I've been in the zoo many weeks now. Weeks since I've been outside these walls.

Inside there's safety. There's Calliope and Leda, Tina and Kyle, my cage and my key. Outside are Aunt Phoebe's tears, Brian's punches, and a house where ghostly movies play inside my head. Outside are photographs, and those who look at them.

Outside is a name, my name. A name I let someone steal away from me.

I take a step back and savor the relief, then two steps forward and savor the nervous energy rushing through me, savor the million voices in my head shouting "No!", because that's a part of the journey too.

I move forward. I take backward steps too, when the voices get to me. Still, I'm moving closer. Step by step. There is no other way to make a journey.

The exit has a revolving gate. I put my hand on the metal. Cool, scratched, dented from years of use. All I need to do is push, to take one more step. The way out is the only way back inside.

I tighten my grip on the gate, tense my arm, lean forward, and prepare to push.

Inside there's Leia. Outside there's me.